# THROUGH THE FIVE HOLE

S.L. STERLING

Through the Five Hole

Copyright © 2025 by S.L. Sterling

All rights reserved. Without limiting the rights under copyright reserved about, no part of this publication may be reproduced, stored in, or introduced into a retrieval system, or transmitted in any form or by any means (mechanical, electronic, photocopying, recording, or otherwise) without the prior written permission of both the copyright owner and the above publisher of the book. This is a work of fiction. Any references to historical events, real people, or real places are used fictitiously. Other names, characters, places, and events are products of the author's imagination, and any resemblance to actual events or places or persons, living or dead, is entirely coincidental. Disclaimer: This book contains mature content not suitable for those under the age of 18. It involves strong language and sexual situations. All parties portrayed in sexual situations are consenting adults over the age of 18.

ISBN: 978-1-998649-01-3

Paperback ISBN: 978-1-998649-22-8

Editor: Brandi Aquino, Editing Done Write

Cover Design: Thunderstruck Cover Design

# Chapter One

Colton - Three Days Later After Arrest

I COULD HEAR the murmur of voices through the window. My head was pounding as I sat up and glanced through the small bedroom window. The entire team sat in the backyard, talking among themselves, surely about what had happened earlier this week.

I kicked the blankets off me and stood up, stretched, and then looked around for my shorts and T-shirt. Surely, they were in here somewhere, I thought to myself, moving a box that had Knox's name on it to see if they had fallen behind. When I didn't find them there, I turned to check the other side of the bedroom and saw a piece of paper on top of the dresser.

I washed the clothes you were wearing. They were filthy, stunk even, figured you'd like something clean. You can find them hanging in the laundry room. ~ Lorelai

Knox had picked me up from the police station late last night and insisted on bringing me here to stay with him and Lorelai. I'd have preferred if he'd just taken me home, that way I could mentally kick myself in peace, but he'd said Lorelai insisted. It wasn't every day one of us spent a couple of nights in jail, and according to Knox, she was worried about me.

I made my way down the hall, stopping at the laundry room door to find my T-shirt and shorts neatly folded on the dryer. Grabbing them, I quickly dressed before making my way to the backyard. I glanced out the door to see the guys all huddled together, but the moment they heard the squeak from the door, they broke apart and looked my way.

I made my way over to the only empty chair off to the side and sat down.

"Don't let my being here ruin whatever it is you were saying," I muttered, reaching down and grabbing one beer from the cooler that was beside the chair.

I'd just cracked it open when the cold can was

ripped from my hand, and I looked up to see Lorelai standing in front of me.

"What do you think you are doing?" I questioned.

She didn't back down from me; instead, she stood there, meeting my eyes.

"Colton, I'm sorry, but I will not allow you to ruin your career. The other night was…well…it was enough."

"It was a minor hiccup." I shrugged. "Now please, I'd like that drink."

"A minor hiccup? You got arrested!"

Every one of these guys knew not to put me in a corner and could probably tell from the look on my face she was doing exactly that. Not that I'd ever hurt her; hell, she was the entire reason I was in this mess. The media would have destroyed her and Knox, and there was no way I was going to allow one of my best friends to lose the best thing that ever happened to him because of some smug, lying reporter. They'd do anything for a story.

Instead of saying anything or fighting with her, I reached down into the cooler, grabbed another can, cracked it open, and took a swig.

"Colton, does this look like a minor hiccup to you?" Knox said, coming over, dropping a newspaper on my lap and taking the beer from my hand.

I went to grab the beer back but missed, then took

notice of the headline on the front of the sports page: *Vancouver Dominator's Bad Boy at it Again, Colton Fox has been arrested, charges pending.*

As I stared at the newspaper, my stomach turned. While I'd been in my fair share of trouble, I'd never pushed it so far as to be arrested or charged with anything. I looked up at Knox to have him shove his cell phone at me, showing me an article on one of the sports apps, stating that Lorelai and I were involved.

"He printed it anyway, that fucker. Fuck, Knox, you better not believe that shit? That right there is what I was trying to stop," I said, looking up at him.

"No, of course I don't believe it."

"We are worried about you," Aurora added.

"Yeah, man, we really are worried," Brad, one of the younger members of the team, said.

"There isn't anything to be worried about. This, like all the others, will blow over."

"I don't know. When I spoke to Larson and Thompkins, they were furious," Dylan said, standing up from where he was sitting while holding Jackson.

I pinched the bridge of my nose.

"You spoke to Larson and Thompkins?"

"Yeah, of course. So did Lorelai and Knox. We needed to get the teams' lawyers involved. Pamela knows too. They needed to know what happened."

"Fuck my life," I muttered under my breath.

Since I'd spent the last couple of nights in jail and still hadn't been home, I didn't know if they had tried to call me. I could only imagine they had.

"Oh god," I heard Lucas gasp.

"What?" Knox questioned, turning around.

"I just got a text from Ella."

Ella was Lucas's wife and worked in the Dominators Promotions department. If that wasn't bad enough, she was also Larson's daughter. Ella hadn't been around because she'd been taking care of her grandmother, taking her back and forth to cancer treatment; she'd probably already heard about the situation.

"And?" Lorelai questioned.

"Ella just got an email from Larson. She says she doesn't want to get involved, but we should check out the *Ice Insiders* app."

"I'm not looking at that drivel," Levi said, pulling his phone from his pocket.

"Neither am I," Scarlett added, shifting Mia from one side of her lap to the other. "You guys know what kind of garbage they publish."

"Check The Blue Line Bulletin," Clay suggested.

"Yes, that will give you the most up-to-date information," Dylan said, winking at Scarlett.

Scarlett had worked for the *Ice Insiders*, and it soon came to light how much they loved to ruin anyone, so I could only imagine what was being printed about me there.

"What does it say?" I questioned.

The entire team checked their phones, each one of them staring at the screen for a few seconds before looking over at me.

"Well, is someone going to enlighten me?"

"They've suspended you from the team." Lorelai gasped. "Effective immediately. The article was published last night."

I reached into my pocket and pulled out my phone, quickly checking my email. What she was saying was true. Larson himself had emailed me with their decision; I'd just chosen to ignore it until I was in a better frame of mind.

"What about the playoffs?" Levi questioned. "We need him, Dylan."

"I know I can always talk to Thompkins, ask him to talk to Larson to reconsider his decision until after the playoffs," Dylan added.

"Dylan, don't get involved. It looks like you'll all have to do without me, boys. The email from Larson states they will determine my fate at the beginning of next season. Until then, I'm not to step foot in the arena aside from working out and for practice. It doesn't even say whether I can go to the games."

"That's bullshit. I'll talk with him," Dylan said, handing Jackson to Aurora.

"No, I did this. I'll take the heat. I'll go in and talk with him, and if they decide to pitch me at the beginning of next season, they do." I shrugged.

"No, Colton, I'll talk with them," Lorelai said.

I got up from the chair I was sitting in. "No, sweetheart, you won't. I did this. I own up to it."

"You were only protecting me."

"Exactly, and I'd do it all over again in a heartbeat. Now, if you guys will excuse me, I think I'm gonna head on home."

Lorelai looked up at me with tears in her eyes.

"No worries, sweets, things always have a way of working out." I leaned down and placed a kiss on her cheek, gave Knox a fist bump, and left the backyard while waving to the others. As I made my way to the front of the house to where my truck was, I hoped I was right. I hoped things would work out because, for the first time in my entire career, I was actually happy where I was.

## Chapter Two

Emma - End of August

I'D WOKEN WITH A HEADACHE, like most Monday mornings lately. It was probably because of the change in weather. Days were cooler and were getting shorter. I poured the hot water into my mug, the smell of spearmint already dulling the pain I was feeling searing through my temples. I picked up my mug and wandered back to the bedroom, where the business news was just ending on the TV. I set my mug down and grabbed the remote, turning the TV down, and made my way over to the bed where I'd placed the two skirts I had chosen for today.

I picked up one skirt and held it up against the

blouse I'd chosen, and that was when I glanced over at the TV to see that the sports news was starting, so I grabbed the remote and turned the TV off, turning my attention back to my outfit. When I finally decided, I slipped into it and then carried my mug into the bathroom.

I glanced at myself in the mirror and placed my mug down on the counter. I couldn't help but notice the bags under my eyes as I reached for my concealer. While I was happy the summer was over, in some ways I wished it could start all over again. We'd had one of the busiest summers ever, hosting dinners and visiting with friends, but as a couple, we'd had one of our worst. The arguing and fighting only got worse the deeper into summer we went.

"Emma, don't forget we have dinner this weekend with the Chilton's," I heard Mark yell from the bedroom.

I sighed and rolled my eyes. This was the fifth time he'd reminded me in three days. Ignoring him, I swiped my eyeshadow on, carefully blending the color, and then doing the same on the other eyelid.

"Did you hear me?" Mark said, poking his head into the bathroom, smacking his hand on the door-frame, the noise causing pain to shoot through my temples.

"I heard you" I sighed. "Dinner this weekend with

the Chilton's," I said, not bothering to look at him in the mirror.

Why hadn't he left for work yet? He'd offered to drive me to the office, but I'd declined when he told me he was planning on leaving early. Besides, I'd rather walk than get involved in another early-morning argument regarding the lack of bedroom activities. He'd complained about that enough over the entire summer.

"I noticed when I mentioned it to you the other day you didn't put it in your calendar, and I just don't want you to forget. This dinner is important," he said, grabbing his suit jacket off the door handle and quickly putting it on, then adjusting his collar and tie. "This deal is important. I know this dinner is going to wrap it up."

"I know, Mark, I won't forget."

"Whatever," Mark mumbled under his breath.

I huffed.

"Tell me when I've ever forgotten?" I muttered, annoyance filling me.

This was how things had been between us lately. We didn't out and out argue; it was just underhanded comments and remarks to one another to get at one another. Each of us would get defensive, and then after a while we'd fight.

"I'm not saying you forget," he said, coming up

beside me, grabbing his cologne and giving himself a generous spritz.

"Then what are you saying?" I questioned.

"All I said was that I noticed you didn't put it in your calendar."

"I don't see the need to put it in my calendar when all you do is harp on me about not forgetting. I've heard all about this dinner for the past two or three weeks. It's hard to forget about something when it's being shoved in your face every minute of every day."

"Fine, I won't mention it again."

I watched as he picked up his razor, bringing it to his cheek and lightly shaving a spot that didn't even need to be shaved.

"What time will you be home tonight?" I questioned, putting on my eyeliner.

"It will be late. I've got an action-packed day. What about you?"

I shrugged, grabbing my lip gloss. "I'm not really working on anything at the moment, so I might have an early night."

"Well, don't wait up. It will probably be close to ten or eleven before I get in. I'm having dinner tonight with the partners and will probably have work to do after that. I'm late, I have to go, and you'd better get a move on or else you're going to be late as well. Are you sure you don't want me to drive you in?"

"I'm sure." I sighed, closing my eyes as Mark pressed a kiss to my cheek and then took off out of the bathroom, grabbing his laptop bag as he went.

The moment I heard the front door close, I felt the tension in my body release. For the past month, I'd constantly felt as if I were walking on eggshells around him, which wasn't how a relationship was supposed to be.

I let out a sigh, swiped some gloss across my lips, and then took off out of the bathroom, grabbing my laptop as I went down the stairs and ate my breakfast in peace.

WITH MY COFFEE IN HAND, I opened the large glass doors of the building I worked in. I greeted Jeff, the security guard, while dropping a small brown bag on his desk while he was on the phone, and then made my way over to the elevator.

"Thanks, Emma!" I heard and turned to see him holding up the brown bag.

"No problem. It's your favorite muffin, Morning Glory, as always."

"You're the best." He waved.

I took the elevator up to the twenty-fifth floor and walked out of the elevator to see the familiar sign reading Image Hackers on the wall. I opened the office door and made my way inside, walking through the office. It was busy this morning, but I still heard the low mumbles surrounding me as I made my way to my corner office.

I rarely paid any attention to anyone in this office, but this morning those same inaudible murmurs I heard bothered me. My co-workers deemed me the Ice Queen because I treated each case with a lack of emotion and precision, like a surgeon. They also didn't like the fact that I kept my private life private, which gave them less to talk about.

Not that there was much to talk about. Our private life was dead. Mark and I never went on double dates; we also didn't participate in any office events with this office. With the amount of gossip that went on here, I'd had no other choice than to pull away, especially after the great scandal sheet that went around. Actually, with the amount of gossip that goes on in any office, it should be enough to make everyone realize the importance of keeping important things private.

Then, sometimes I wondered if gossip might not spice things up between us. I wasn't happy with how things were, just like he wasn't, but the truth was we were both married to our jobs. The only dates we ever went on now were with his clients, which were always business related, and recently he'd stopped asking me to go with him on those unless it was an important dinner like this weekend because he claimed I was too busy with work to attend most times. Which honestly wasn't a lie.

I placed my coffee down on my desk, pulled my laptop from my bag, and began setting up my desk, getting myself prepared for what I hoped was a busy week. I was just about to check my email when I heard a tiny knock on my door, and I looked up to see Jane standing there, a small smile on her face.

"Morning, Emma. I just wanted to let you know Kerry has asked to see you. She has an assignment for you."

"Oh, wonderful. Do you know the details?" I asked, excited to learn more.

Jane shook her head. "All she said was that it was massively important, and she wants to see you immediately."

"Okay," I said, frowning as I grabbed my notebook and pen.

Five minutes later, I walked into Kerry's office and took a seat across from her. I smoothed my skirt, then crossed my legs, opened my notebook, and got ready to make notes as I always did.

"You can put your notebook down," she said,

opening her top drawer, pulling out a file, which she placed on her desk, and then clasped her hands together in front of her.

"I've been working on some things for the past month, and this morning I got the call with permission to move ahead. I need someone to take on a rather urgent case."

"I'm all ears." I smiled.

"It's a do-or-die sort of case, and you are the only person in this entire office I can trust enough to take this on. In trust, I mean holding yourself out there to represent this company the way you always do, but also, to keep things private for the sake of the client."

"Wow, okay, well you've piqued my curiosity," I said, smiling, knowing immediately it must be someone with a high public profile.

"I'm glad. It's not just the case. I owe someone a huge favor, and when this came across my desk originally, I knew it was my way to pay them back. Under no circumstances can this fail."

I sat up a little straighter, noting the look in Kerry's eyes. She wasn't joking around; she was serious.

"Of course. I'll do whatever it is, and you know I'll take it seriously. You can trust me on that," I replied. "I love working for Image Hackers, and I always handle every case with discretion and professionalism," I said.

"I know. That was why I immediately thought of

you this morning when I got the approval," she said, getting up and going over to her small coffee station, pouring two cups and bringing them back over to her desk, placing one cup in front of me. "It also works perfectly since you've finished your entire caseload and are completely clear for a while."

"Thank you, yes, I worked hard to get all the loose ends wrapped up in a timely manner so I could start fresh in the fall, although the cases weren't that challenging, but they are all finished now," I said, taking a sip.

"Well, I hate to say it, but this one might be a little different from the others. Tell me, what do you know about hockey star Colton Fox?"

I swallowed hard. "Colton Fox?" I asked.

"Yes, Colton Fox."

Almost immediately, all I could see were his stunning glass-blue eyes looking at me before he walked away from me. There was no way this was the same Colton Fox, I thought as I sat there internally and silently praying that it wasn't the same guy I'd known from childhood.

"Not much, why?"

Kerry pulled out a pile of photographs from the folder in front of her and placed them on the desk, along with a pile of newspaper clippings, spreading them out for me to see.

I flipped through them all, then through the pictures, swallowing hard. Pictures of him coming out of clubs with women draped all over him, walking out of casinos flipping the bird to the camera, then more pictures of him with women. The article headlines were crazy, some dealing with gambling issues, relationship issues that ranged anywhere from public breakups to one-night stands, and a whack of articles suggesting anger issues.

I picked up another image of Colton. It most definitely was the same Colton Fox, and suddenly I regretted being so eager to take on this case.

"I don't understand? Where is the urgency? These articles are dated more than a year ago, most from when he was playing for his last team. There is nothing recent that I can see," I said, my jaw tight as I dropped the photograph onto the desk.

"That's right, but about six months ago, Colton Fox was traded to the Vancouver Dominators. Prior to that move, he'd been cleaning up his act, and everything was going okay, until the very end of last season."

I sat there watching as Kerry pulled out another folder and placed it down in front of me. I opened the folder to see a picture of Colton and a beautiful woman in front of a house, both of them looking toward the camera. I shuffled to the next page, and that was when I saw the first article. *Could it be true?*

*Evans Girl leaving him for the new Bad Boy of the team.* Then I flipped to the next article. *Vancouver Dominator's Bad Boy at it Again, Colton Fox arrested for assault, charges pending, Once a Player always a Player, hockey's notorious bad boy at it again.*

"Did he beat her?" I questioned, wondering where the assault charge was coming from.

"Nope, he attacked the paparazzi that were outside his home. Apparently, the woman pictured here not only works for the team but is also involved in a serious relationship with Knox Evans, another Dominator."

"Are these two involved with one another?" I asked.

"Nope. When I spoke with the PR team, they said Lorelai Anderson was taking Colton home after a night out with the team. She'd walked with him to the door to make sure he was okay getting in the house, and that was when the reporters approached. Colton apparently didn't want them there and told them to leave, and they started asking him questions about the two of them, probing for information. I guess Miss Anderson tried to take control of the situation and told them to leave, but they refused. They requested an interview, and when Fox refused, they threatened they were going to slander her all over the paper. They began taking pictures of the two of them together, and that was when Colton flew off the handle, attacking the photographer, breaking his camera, and then he turned on the reporter. The photographer had his nose broken but crawled away and called the police. The reporter wasn't as lucky—broken hand, broken arm."

I sat back in the chair and skimmed through the second article while Kerry continued.

"Basically, Mr. Fox's agent has hired this firm to help clean up his image."

I placed the articles back on her desk and looked at Kerry. "How are we supposed to do that?"

"I'm glad you asked. While Mr. Fox has had a lot of issues in the past with gambling and relationships, the team he was with prior to the Dominators forced him to go to Gamblers Anonymous, which cleaned up a pile of the relationship issues. However, the anger issues are another matter. The headlines keep coming as well, stating that Fox and Miss. Anderson are in fact involved. The most recent one being pictures of Mr. Fox leaving her office after physio treatment for a bit of back injury he suffered while in the gym, and any other images they have their hands on where the two of them are near one another. That needs to stop."

"That part is simple. I've got my media contacts, but I am not sure what I am supposed to do about the other, unless Mr. Fox agrees to go to anger management."

"I'm glad you asked. Mr. Fox's agent and the PR team for the Dominators have agreed that he would take part in anger management, which he just completed. They have also hired us to introduce to the media and the world the secret girlfriend of Mr. Colton Fox."

"Ah, gotcha. So, you want me to find someone to fill that position, let it play out for a while, build up Mr. Fox's reputation in public, and then quietly end things between the two of them in the spotlight. It's doable. I mean, everyone loves a love story. I'm just trying to think of who I'd get to play the part."

I picked up my coffee mug and took a mouthful of coffee, making a couple of notes in my book as I thought about which girl I could use. There was Vicki. I hadn't used her in one of my cases in a while, or I could always call Violet. She was always up for a challenge, and she normally only worked on low-profile cases, ones that weren't involved with the media, normally private, office-related issues with CEOs.

"Exactly. I want the world to see them together. I want the world to see the real Mr. Colton Fox, but I don't want you to hire someone."

Kerry paused as I finished my notes.

"What?" I said as I looked up from my notebook, waiting for her to continue. "I need to hire someone if I am going to be successful," I reminded her. "Unless he already has a girlfriend and you just want me to oversee the events they participate in, maybe arrange some interviews or some charity work. Events and dinners are always a good option as well."

"Emma, there is no girlfriend. We aren't using one of our girls. I've decided that I am putting you in charge of this case – only you. That means you are to move in with Mr. Fox, attend games, events, and the like while helping to clean up his image. You are to play his other half."

The room stilled as I looked at her. I could have cut the air in the room with a knife.

"I'm sorry, but I thought I heard you say you wanted me to move in with Mr. Fox." I chuckled.

"That's correct. Mr. Fox has just completed his suspension and will start playing at the season's opener. He has appearances to make, interviews, charity dinners and the like. The first one being Saturday in three weeks. The goal is to have his reputation cleaned and repaired by the end of the year. If not by then, before the playoffs."

"Kerry, while I'm flattered that you want me to handle this, and I don't have any issues doing so, my job is to organize and oversee these sorts of situations, not to actually be a part of them."

"I understand that, but you have to understand. This is for a dear friend of mine, and I need you to step up and take full control. Plus, with Mr. Fox being in the spotlight, it needs to be a woman we've never used before. We deal with a lot of high-end clients, and most of the girls we hire are in the public eye—they won't work for this case."

"That was why I thought of Violet."

"No, Violet won't do. She isn't the type of girl that could handle this. You are, and that is why I trust only you. So, that being said, you will fly out in three weeks. You will arrive in Vancouver at approximately eleven. Someone from the Dominators will be at the airport to pick you up to take you to the arena, and the PR team will take it from there, as will you."

Kerry pulled out an envelope, passing it to me, which I opened to see a plane ticket in my name to Vancouver.

"How long do you figure I'll be gone?" I questioned.

"As long as it takes but count on at least until December. Possibly that timeline could extend. I've heard that Mr. Fox can be a little difficult."

I nodded, getting up from the chair I was sitting on. There was no use in trying to get my way. I knew Kerry had already decided.

"May I take these?" I asked, nodding to the folders on the desktop. "I just want to look things over, to form my plan of attack. Also, get an idea of what it is I'm walking into."

"Of course. Good luck, and, Emma, do me proud."

I'd returned to my desk and sat down to go through all the information when my phone buzzed. I grabbed it to see a message from my best friend Chantal, whom I'd known since high school. A smile came to my face as I opened our chat.

Chantal: How did the rest of the weekend go after I left on Wednesday night?

I SMILED. Chantal had come over to join me for dinner and had just been getting ready to leave when Mark arrived home. Chantal was a couple's therapist and someone I'd expressed my concerns to about my relationship with Mark. She'd listened to me and then gave me some pointers, and she'd told me she'd be following up with me today to see how things had gone.

Emma: Same as always, no change, and this morning we got into it about that stupid dinner with the Chiltons.

Chantal: Again?

Emma: Of course, again. He's always on me about that dinner. Thinking I'll forget.

Chantal: Did you ask him why? Like I suggested.

Emma: I did, but it doesn't matter; he believes what he wants anyway.

Chantal: Well, we could always set up a time for the three of us to sit down and talk it through.

Emma: You know his feelings on that.

Chantal: Sadly yes, I do. I'm here if you want to talk. Anything else exciting going on?

Emma: Yep, work calls. I've been assigned to a high-profile case out of town.

Chantal: Oh, don't you work only from this office?

Emma: Usually yes. Okay, I have to tell you, but it needs to stay here.

Chantal: Of course, you don't need to worry.

Emma: It's Colton Fox

Chantal: Um…as in the Colton Fox

Emma: Yes

Chantal: Oh Emma, are you going to be alright?

Emma: Will I be alright? Of course, I will be.

Chantal: Yeah, but…Jesus, you have…

Emma: Don't, okay, Don't remind me.

Chantal: Someone needs to…

Emma: Listen, I promise I'll be okay. I'm not that little girl anymore.

# Chapter Three

Colton - End of August

"I KNEW this day would come, and honestly I'm amazed it wasn't sooner."

I was pretty sure the vein on Thompkins' forehead was about to burst as he paced back and forth in front of me.

"I don't understand why you are such a fuck-up!" he screamed, bringing me right back to my childhood.

I'd learned a long time ago, it was better to keep my mouth shut than it was to open it and start fighting back or trying to defend myself. Plus, I'd heard this lecture before. It wouldn't matter the reason I'd lost my temper, because he'd never listen to me anyway.

"I'm pretty sure that when you came here, it was written in your contract in clear English that you were to keep your act clean. This isn't fucking clean! In fact, it seems to get worse the longer time goes on," he said, throwing down a copy of a sports article I'd not yet seen.

I reached for the paper, reading the headline: *Once a Player, Always a Player, Hockey's Notorious Bad Boy's Secret Affair.* Slamming the article down on the desktop, I started smirking at the fact that they were still going on about this.

"What the fuck do you find funny?" Thompkins screamed, getting right down into my face.

"This is ridiculous. I was simply defending Lorelai, so they wouldn't drag her name through the mud. Besides, they shouldn't have been lurking outside my house. Now they are lurking in this very building, capturing pictures they have no right to capture on private property while I'm in treatment for my back, and you aren't doing a single thing about it."

"Well, I see you clearly accomplished what you set out to do. As for the lurking, there are many other ways to deal with that than to beat the shit out of two reporters."

"Well, they pissed me off!" I yelled back. "Accusing us of having an affair. Besides, it's been two months. They really need to lay the fuck off."

"So what? They pissed you off, big deal. You know what pisses me off? Players like you who only think about themselves. In that moment, there were so many other things you could have done to deal with the situation."

"Like what?"

"Well, for starters, being sober would have been one of them! Or you could have done as Lorelai suggested and gone into the house, allowed her to call us, and allowed us to deal with it. Instead, you took matters into your own hands, leaving the girl in a poor panic, making a mess of everything you've worked hard to undo."

I sat slumped in the chair, listening to every word Thompkins said. While part of me really didn't care what I'd done, I knew he was right. After a public apology, The Enforcers had forced me into Gamblers Anonymous three years ago, and while it had been the best thing to cure my gambling addiction, it had also cured the women it drew as well. While the guys all thought my bedroom was active as hell and I had plenty of women at my beck and call, they didn't know the half of it. My private life was dead, completely dried up. In fact, I hadn't had action in so long, I was thinking I'd be giving away my virginity again when the time came—not that I'd ever tell them that though.

"Nothing has been undone. I'm not out gambling,

I'm not out being photographed with inappropriate women as my last coach called them—"

"No, you are right. Instead, you were out beating the shit out of photographers and reporters because they used the thought of you and Lorelai to get a reaction out of you."

"Yep, and thanks to that decision, which I'm really not proud of, I have completed the anger management sessions that Larson asked to take, and I have completed the terms of my suspension, not breaking a single rule."

Thompkins shook his head and leaned over me. "You have fucked your career and this team, Colton, and you did it all right in the middle of the fucking playoffs. Just be thankful I've had a couple of months to cool off."

I glared at him, causing him to back off me. He didn't need to tell me what I already knew. The team had been counting on me. I knew that, and I'd let them down. I knew that too. It was thanks to me and my poor decisions that had cost us our chance at winning the cup.

"I haven't fucked my career. I'll be in the spotlight for a while, until another player does something more outrageous than this. Give it time. It will blow over. It always does."

"Well, according to your theory, in the three

months you guys have been off, someone should have done something more outrageous than you have, yet here we are. The articles are still pouring in."

That was when the office door opened and Larson walked in, followed by Pamela and my agent, Kent. This day just got better, I thought to myself.

The room was silent as the three of them walked in. Two of them made themselves comfortable in chairs before they all turned their attention to me, none of them smiling, while Larson walked over to Thompkins and mumbled something at him.

Kent looked at me, then reached for a file, standing up.

"Colton, effective Thursday, your team suspension is over. However, your contract is still under review, pending the outcome of the pending charges. When the Dominators signed you, there was an agreement that you didn't drag your shit here. You have broken that agreement, so they have asked to have some time to rethink their decision to allow you to remain with the team. They have until the end of the season to decide, which if they want you to leave, would make you a free agent."

I looked over at Larson and Thompkins. Both men stood there staring straight at me with the same look I'd seen from the Enforcers' owners and coach had when they'd announced they were trading me.

"That being said, with the suspension this summer and your contract under review, your sponsors were going to drop you, but I was able to convince them not to because I told them you would not only fulfill your contract with each of them but you were taking steps to fix this mess. They have agreed to resign again next season, but only if you clean up your act and stay on with the Dominators."

It was then that Pamela cleared her throat and looked at me.

"What? How am I to clean up my act?" I shrugged. "I think it's pretty safe to say that maybe Thompkins and everyone else is right. Maybe I am just a fuckup."

I'd heard those words from my father right until I'd eventually moved out of his home. I was almost certain those were the words he'd uttered as he waved to me as I backed out of his driveway, and if I were honest, they were also the exact words he muttered to me right before he passed away.

"You aren't a fuckup, and we aren't just giving up on you, Colton. You have completed the things that we have asked so far, and you have obeyed all aspects of your suspension. That speaks volumes, but we want to make sure this topic doesn't come back up and that you are only highlighted in a positive light in the future. So, we have come up with a solution to fix this mess, but it's one that is not up for discussion or negotiation," Larson said, crossing his arms in front of him, letting me know he meant what he said.

I looked over at Pamela, who shuffled through some papers before finally stopping. She looked at me, an unsettling look in her eyes.

"We have hired a personal PR campaign person to be assigned to you."

"What?" I questioned.

The Enforcers had tried this before. I'd given it my best shot, but I was also going through a rough time. My dad was dying, my mom had just gotten her cancer diagnosis, and I refused to allow anyone in because, in my eyes, no one understood what I was going through. Granted, things had changed now, but despite that, I am a grown ass man, I didn't want a babysitter.

"She will be here in three weeks, and—"

I stood up, stopping Pamela. "I'll be damned if I am going to be babysat by some PR nightmare. Been there, done that, probably still have the fucking T-shirt."

"Sit the fuck down!" Thompkins yelled.

I glanced at Thompkins and then sat back down in the chair and looked at Pamela.

"You will! She will be here with you until the end of the year, and if that doesn't do it, until the end of the season."

Every nerve in my body was on fire. What kind of bullshit was this? "What exactly do you mean by staying with me?"

"Colton, have you heard of a company by the name Image Hackers?" Pamela asked.

I shook my head.

"They are a company that focuses on repairing the image of public figures. They are excellent at what they do, and we have hired the best of the best."

I rolled my eyes and sat back, waiting to hear what sort of garbage idea they were actually trying to force me into participating in.

"Uh-huh, go on," I said, crossing my arms.

"I want to introduce you to Emma, your new girl-friend," Pamela said, standing up and holding out a piece of paper for me to take.

"Fuck that!" I said, shoving the paper back at her without even looking at it and standing up.

"Colton, sit back down, NOW!" Larson yelled.

I couldn't help but chuckle. "Not a chance! This meeting is over. You're all welcome to sit here and dream up the next bullshit idea you think I'll fall for, but please, only call me when it's a decent idea."

I flew out of the office, anger coursing through me. I was just about at the end of the hall when I heard my name and turned to see Kent following me.

"Leave me alone, Kent!" I yelled back, continuing

down the hall. "I don't want to talk. I'm not in the mood."

I opened the doors leading to the locker rooms when I felt a hand on my shoulder. "What?" I said, whipping around.

"Colton, I think it would be best if you at least gave this solution a try," Kent said, taking a step back and giving me some space.

"You do, do you?"

"Yeah, I do."

"I've done everything they've wanted, but I'm not doing this. This is just over the top."

"Look, I know it will be a pain in the ass to have someone at your side all the time, but honestly, this is one surefire way to get your image cleaned up. It will give you a chance to show your fans and the public the real you. Then, once it is over, you can continue to build a better image of yourself. It's a short-term solution with a long-term promise that will pay off for you in the end."

"How do you figure?"

"This company is excellent, and the person they have agreed to send truly is one of their best. I'd never ask this if I didn't believe it myself, so I am asking you to reconsider. Otherwise, I'm afraid I won't be able to get them to agree to keep you here."

"Reconsider? You are serious?"

"Yes, Colton, I'm afraid I am. I was the one who brought this idea to them. They were going to drop you immediately after last season. I had to beg them to listen. A good friend of mine runs Image Hackers, and I know her work. I trust her. It will be discreet and private. No one will know the truth except for us and those you choose to tell."

I stood in the hallway, looking my agent square in the eyes as I considered his words. I'd trusted Kent my entire career. He'd been with me since I started playing professionally. He'd been with me when my dad kicked me out, he'd been there for me when he died, and again when my mother died and I was alone. In ways, Kent was more than an agent; he'd become family and probably one of the few people I could trust and count on.

"Are you sure this will work?" I questioned.

"I'd never have suggested it if I'd doubted it would work," he said with confidence.

I thought for a moment. If Larson or Thompkins had brought this to me, there was no way in hell I'd even consider it.

"Fine. Tell them fine," I said, feeling defeated.

"Colton, I promise you, this will work. Since you have been out of the negative spotlight for so long, this should have blown over quickly. We've concocted the story that you've broken up with your long-time girlfriend, Emma, and that is why you've gotten into hot water. We've already submitted the interview with you announcing the breakup and what led you to your decisions that night, and next we are going to start with your reconnection."

I pinched the bridge of my nose and shook my head. "You did what? What interview?" I questioned.

"Just calm down. I provided the answers for the interview."

"Even my agent betrays me?" I questioned.

"I've done everything for you. The article will go to print today."

"Great, I can't wait to read it."

"I focused mostly on the heartbreak you felt that led you to make that decision that night."

I shook my head in disbelief. "What am I, twelve? Oh, and newsflash, I've dated no one that the public knows about. The only girls I've been photographed with were the girls associated with my gambling addiction."

"We're aware. We are still working on the details, but I assure you we took all of that into consideration. Once she arrives, we will get photographs of the two of you in a public setting and release the next article about rekindling."

"I see. Boy, you guys have really thought this through."

"I was up all hours last night on a conference call with Emma figuring this out."

"Oh, I bet you were." I sighed.

"You will make a public announcement at the opening dinner apologizing to the team and your teammates and to the public. Then, at some point, we will do an in-home shoot with you and Emma."

"Why would we do an in-home shoot?"

Kent shifted from foot to foot while looking at me.

"Well, they will want to capture images of you and Emma together," he answered. "Everyone loves a love story, especially one they can be a part of. Our aim is to get you going viral on all Puck-Lit-Love pages."

"What the hell is that?" I questioned.

"Well, it's super popular according to Emma. It is a forum that brings romance readers together for their love of hockey, and since we want to target the female population a little more because of the angle we are aiming at, when she suggested it, I thought it was brilliant."

"Uh-huh, I bet you did." I moaned, rolling my eyes. "I'm still failing to understand why they would capture pictures at my home if I'm out in the public with her?"

Kent let out a sigh. "Colton, I know it won't be easy having a stranger living in your home, but—"

"Whoa, wait a minute, who the hell said anything

about her living in my home? She's here to do a few photo ops, attend a few games, and that is all."

"No, Colton, this has to be real. It has to be believable. I think it's safe to say that if you were in a relationship with someone for six years, you'd have her stay at your home, not in a hotel."

"Yep, that is probably a safe assumption—assuming I am dating someone, but I'm not. Why don't you just tell the media I had a moment of poor judgment. Jesus," I said, running my fingers through my hair. "That will be more believable than this facade."

"Colton, we need to fix this. We need to reinvent your image. People cannot be afraid of you, and right now, they are. So, we need you to show tenderness, compassion and…a very human side of you."

"To a fake-ass relationship," I said, irritated that I'd allowed this conversation to continue.

"You need to let people in, show them your personal side, let them know about the charity work—"

Immediately, I held my hand out, shutting him up. "Don't you dare bring that up," I said through clenched teeth, glaring at him.

Kent froze and took a step back before clearing his throat.

"I swear, if I find out you mentioned anything about that in this so-called interview you forged, I'll fire your ass."

"You're right, I should know better than to mention that. I promise I mentioned nothing about it."

"Damn right you should."

"We're good, right?" Kent questioned, still unsure if I was going to back out or stay the course with their ridiculous idea.

"Yep, we are good."

"Okay, great, now I need to get back in there and tell them you are agreeing to this. I need you to clean up your guest bedroom, get some groceries, get some furniture, and get ready for one busy fall season."

"Yep, whatever," I said, taking off through the door on my way to the locker room.

# Chapter Four

Emma - Late September

WITH MY BAG slung over my shoulder and a cafe mocha in my hand, I boarded the plane that was heading to Vancouver. The last three weeks had been hell. While I'd been working on getting things ready for this case, Mark had been planning his exit. It was right after the dinner with the Chilton's, and my announcement that I'd be leaving for a minimum of three months for work, that he announced that he'd met someone. A week later, he'd moved himself along with all his things in with Bianca, his administrative assistant. While at first I'd been upset, it was Chantal who quickly reminded me how unhappy I was.

I'd just gotten everything arranged at my seat and had sat down when I felt my phone vibrate. I grabbed it and looked down to see a message from Chantal.

Chantal: Good luck with everything. ;)

Emma: What's the wink for?

Chantal: As if you don't know?

Emma: I haven't a clue.

Chantal: It's a reminder to go after what you really want.

Emma: Well, what I really want is another cafe mocha to get me through this flight but I'm already on the plane and they are getting ready to taxi out, so I don't think a wink is going to do it.

Chantal: Stop, you know what I'm talking about.

Emma: You are crazy if you think there is ever going to be anything between me and Colton.

Chantal: My dear, my mother always said, never say never.

Emma: I'm not even going to dignify
that with an answer. Talk soon.

Chantal: Safe flight. Go get him.

Emma: :S

## EMMA - SEVENTEEN years ago

"OW! LET GO OF MY HAIR!" I screamed as searing
pain ripped through my scalp.

Evil laughter filled my ears as Heidi Pendalton, the
school's only feared female bully, wrapped my tangled
hair around her fist.

"What are you going to do if I don't?" she sneered,
giving another hard tug before finally letting go of the
handful of hair she had.

I backed up and smoothed out my still-tangled hair,
swallowing hard.

"Where did you get that dress, Emma?"

I looked down at the dress I was wearing. Momma
had bought the sunflower material and had made me

the dress as a surprise for my fourteenth birthday a week ago. Sunflowers were my favorite flower, and I'd always wanted a sunflower dress. Momma and I had little, especially after Dad left us, and I knew this material had cost her a pretty penny. I also knew she'd stayed up late many nights working on it after I'd gone to bed. When I opened it, tears had filled my eyes, and I immediately knew I had to wear it for the first week of tenth grade.

I stared at her as she backed me into a corner in the hallway, her evil smile one I would have loved to smack off her face if I wasn't so afraid of the repercussions. Mom had always told me that violence solved nothing, that you got further by talking.

The moment my back was up against the wall, Heidi grabbed hold of my dress and pulled, and that was when I heard the material rip.

"There, now you'll have to go get something other than this ugly piece of crap." She laughed.

I looked down to see that she'd ripped the dress in a place I knew Mom could never fix, and that was when the tears rolled down my cheeks. I feared what Momma would say when she saw the tear in the material.

"Are you really going to stand there and cry about it?" she said, mocking a fake cry and wiping her eyes before she started laughing.

As I looked up at Heidi, at her evil smiling face, trying to figure out how not to cry but get away from her, shock lined her face. Suddenly, she was ripped away from where we stood, and I heard a deep male voice confront her.

"Heidi! How many more times do I need to tell you to stay the fuck away from girls who are new to the school?"

"Ohhh, look, it's the big hockey player." Heidi laughed.

It was then I watched his almost six-foot-tall frame get between her and me. He was intimidating at his full height, his shoulders already broadening as he ambled toward her.

"I told you once. I won't tell you again. Leave the newbies alone, or you're going to have to deal with me. I'm bigger, I'm stronger and, unlike her, I'm not afraid to hurt you."

In a moment, Heidi had picked up her bag, laughing as she made her way down the hall, and ran out the door.

It was then he turned those glass-blue eyes on me. "Are you okay?"

"I...I think so," I said, straightening myself up and fixing my hair.

"She ripped your dress," he said, his eyes meeting mine.

It was at that moment that tears began streaming down my face. My mother had worked so hard on that dress. Without another word, he grabbed me and pulled me into him, hugging me tight.

That was how I met Colton Fox.

WE DATED THROUGHOUT HIGH SCHOOL, and by the start of his senior year, my friend Chantal came to me to tell me we'd be crowned King and Queen at Spring Prom.

As Spring Prom crept up, so did the pressure of taking our relationship to the next step. So, ten weeks prior to the prom, I'd gone out and got my first tattoo, a present for him and something to remind me of Colton Fox forever.

I lay in bed about eight weeks later, my fingers lightly tracing over my left hip bone. I lay there, agonizing as I tried to figure out how and when to tell Colton about the tattoo. Then, as if I were channeling my mother's better-late-than-never motto, I'd decided I'd tell him tomorrow. I wanted him to know about it prior to prom night, where we'd planned on going back to his house after the party since his parents would be out of town.

I placed my hands behind my head and stared up at my dark ceiling, wondering how I'd even bring up the subject, what I'd say. Maybe I'd just show him the tattoo. My stomach tingled with nerves as my mind ran through all the scenarios when I heard a tap, tap on my window.

I sat up, hearing it again. I slipped out of the bed and cracked my blinds. Colton stood below and gave a wave when he saw me.

I held my finger up and then tiptoed to my door, cracking it open. The house was dark. Mom's bedroom door was cracked open, but her light was off, and I could hear her gently snoring. I slipped from my room and down the stairs, avoiding each creaking step, and made my way to the front door, quietly opening it.

The minute I stepped out onto the front porch, Colton was there.

"Hey." I smiled. "Everything okay?"

It wasn't odd that he was here. He'd come over many nights, late, and we'd sit up on the roof of the porch and talk, or we'd sneak into my room and mess around.

Tonight was different. Tonight, the look in his eyes was one I'd never seen before. It appeared he'd been crying.

"Hey, I had to come. I hope I didn't wake your mom," he whispered.

"No, she worked a double shift, so she's sound asleep. What's up?"

"Emma, I don't know how to tell you this," he murmured.

"Just say it, silly." I smiled, placing my hand on his chest.

He looked at me, a serious look in his eyes. "I'm going out of town."

I looked over his shoulder, a smirk coming to my face when I saw his bicycle lying on the front lawn. "Where are you planning to go on your bike?"

He smiled down at me, not with the same smile he normally had when he looked at me. "No, not on my bike. My parents dropped a bomb on me tonight when I came home from practice. They have decided they are going their separate ways."

"What? Colton, I'm so sorry." I sniffed.

I knew all too well how this felt. Dad had left us when I was seven, and even though I understood little of it then, I understood it all too well now.

"Yeah, so I'm going away for a while."

"Why?"

"My mom will have to leave the house and move into a small apartment, and on her salary, those expenses will be enough. She won't be able to afford to put me through hockey, and you know I have my heart set on trying out for a professional team."

"I know, but surely you could get a job to help with things," I suggested.

"I could, but there'd still be no more hockey. There is no way a part-time job at minimum wage would pay for that."

"So, what are you saying?"

"My dad has announced he is moving to Boston. They have a Junior A team there, and he promised me that he'd make things work."

"I don't understand why he can't make things work here." I sniffled.

"Baby girl, we don't have a Junior A team here. So, I'd be moving eventually, probably within the next year or two."

Tears sprang to my eyes and panic set in at the thought of Colton leaving, but I couldn't bring myself to say anything. My throat was so tight it hurt to swallow, and the tightness I felt in my chest at the thought of not seeing him every day was almost enough to kill me.

He pulled me into him, wrapping his arms around me. I wrapped my arms around him, wishing I never had to let go, because I knew that letting go meant I'd never see him again.

"When will you be leaving?" I questioned, sniffling.

"Tomorrow."

Alarm filled me. "Tomorrow? Before the Spring Prom?"

"I'm afraid so. What am I going to do without you?"

It was then I felt him pull away, place his finger under my chin, and lift my head. He bent down, bringing his lips to mine.

"What do you mean, without me? I'm not breaking up with you."

"It sure feels that way." I sniffed, stepping into him and placing my head on his chest.

"Well, I'm not. We aren't breaking up. We are just going to do the long-distance thing for a bit."

"When will I see you again?"

He placed his hands on my cheeks and looked deep into my eyes. "I'll be back to visit my mom after we get settled. We will make it through this, I promise." He brought his lips to mine again, kissing me hard. "I love you."

"I love you too." I sniffled.

"I have to go," he whispered.

He pulled away and took off down the front steps. He stopped and picked up his bike and then glanced over his shoulder at me.

I didn't need to see him to know he was crying

because, in the darkness, I could see his beautiful blue eyes glistening with tears.

"Goodbye, Emma. I'll send you my address. We can mail letters, email, and of course text. Once I have my new school, work, and hockey schedule, I'll get it to you. We will set up our time to spend time together. We will make this work. I promise."

One more kiss and he hopped onto his bike and rang the tiny bell like he always did when he drove away.

THE DINGING SEATBELT signs on the plane pulled me out of my memory, and I looked down at the pile of papers and pictures in front of me.

"Please put your things away, Miss. Make sure your seatbelt in on and that your seat is placed back in an upright position. We are about to land," the flight attendant said to me as she made her way to the next set of seats, repeating the same thing.

My stomach felt off the moment I'd climbed into the limo, and I was almost certain I was about to be sick when it finally pulled in behind the Vancouver arena. The moment we stopped outside the back entrance, someone opened the door for me.

"Welcome, Miss Cooper. You can leave your bags and everything in the back of the limo while you attend your meeting. They are waiting for you," the man who opened the door said to me as he helped me from the car and escorted me to a side door, swiping a key card in front of a pad to open the door.

"If you are wondering, these are the players' private quarters," he said, studying me. "There is no need to worry. No one is here right now. They are all down on the ice for practice. We figured it would be best for you to meet with the owner of the team, Guy Larson, and the head of the PR team before seeing Mr. Fox."

"Thanks," I said, still following him, my mind going over the notes I'd made with my ideas on how to fix things.

As I walked down the hall, my mind flashed to the images and articles I'd read during my flight. My stomach felt like it was on fire, which wasn't like me at all. I'd been up almost all night with an upset stomach. I honestly felt like I was going on my very first date all over again, but I knew it was because I was being thrown back into the life of Colton Fox. Surely, I'd meet him in person and would instantly remember why I came to hate him to begin with. I'd freeze back up and own up to the name I'd been given—Ice Queen.

I focused on the sound of my heels clicking along the floor as we made our way down another hallway, finally stopping outside of Guy Larson's door. Kerry really hadn't told me too many details, stating that I'd find them out once I arrived in Vancouver.

The gentleman I was with knocked on the door, and then cracked it open, announcing my arrival. Immediately, he turned, smiled, and shoved the door open. I stepped inside, coming face-to-face with the owner of the Vancouver Dominators.

"Emma Cooper, I presume," he said, coming around the desk, holding his hand out for me.

I slipped my hand into his, giving him a firm shake just as the door closed.

"Guy Larson. Please come in, please. Take a seat," he said, pulling out the chair on the opposite side of his desk.

"Mr. Larson, it's nice to meet you," I said, sitting down and straightening my skirt, crossing my legs at the ankles.

"Miss Cooper, I'm glad you are here. I hope your flight went well."

"It did, thank you. Quick and easy." I smiled, reaching into my bag to pull out the file.

"Miss Cooper, I wanted to go over some things

before you meet Mr. Fox. Please, first, you can relax, put your notes away," he said, sitting down in his chair.

This wasn't my style. I was all business, but I did as he asked and hesitantly slipped my folder back into my bag and crossed my hands in my lap. This wasn't how I imagined my meeting going with the owner. In fact, I fully intended to walk in here and come face-to-face with Colton Fox. I watched as he pulled two bottles of water from a mini-fridge behind him, placing one on the desk in front of me.

"I'm sure you're thirsty." He nodded to the bottle, which I took. "Miss Cooper, I won't sugarcoat things. Mr. Fox is probably going to be one of your most challenging cases," he began.

I stiffened my back and smiled. "Mr. Larson, I handle these sorts of cases every day. Mr. Fox won't be anything I can't handle, I can assure you."

A smile came to his lips as he looked at me. "While I'd like to believe that, I know my player. He isn't an amiable man to get along with. In fact, it seems like he has given up caring about most things, especially whether he stays here. I just want you to know that if he gives you any type of trouble at all while you are staying with him, I want to know about it immediately."

The room spun out of control. The only words I'd heard were "while you are staying with him." I swallowed hard, hoping that the panic wasn't present on my face.

"I'm sorry, but I thought I heard you say I'd be staying with him?" I questioned, doing my best to keep my voice from quivering.

"Yes, surely, Kerry told you that you'd be moving in with Mr. Fox."

She had mentioned something along those lines, but I'd figured she hadn't meant it in the literal sense.

"Yes, of course," I said, swallowing hard.

"Okay. Well, if he gives you any type of trouble, be it in his own home or at an away event, we are to be notified of it immediately. He's on thin ice with me. No pun intended, and if he doesn't comply with your instructions or your ideas, he may face another suspension, but he will lose his contract, become a free agent, and be sent to another team the second I hear about an opening."

I nodded. "Of course."

The door opened from behind me, and I turned to see another man enter the room, followed by a woman. They both smiled as they entered, and she closed the door behind them.

"Miss Cooper, this is Coach Thompkins. He will be your direct contact, especially on away games, and this is Pamela, head of the PR department. You will report to her as well, laying out the plan that you have to fix this mess, and then working with her to push things out to the media."

I shook both of their hands but jumped when someone pounded on the door.

I turned, looking at Larson to see his face fall as I heard the door open.

"Miss Cooper," Larson said, standing up from his chair, "I'd like to introduce you to Mr. Colton Fox."

My stomach was in knots as I slowly stood up and turned around. The first thing I saw was his chest and broad shoulders, and then my eyes met his. Those familiar glass-blue eyes I'd probably never forget no matter how long it had been, skimmed my body. He looked exactly as I remembered—a little older, but mostly the same. My stomach hitched as I slipped my small hand into his.

"Wow, it's been a long time," Colton whispered, his eyes locked with mine, a hint of something dancing in his eyes.

The room was silent, and I knew they were watching, so I cleared my throat and straightened my back. This wasn't the time to show any sort of weakness, or to allow anyone in this room to know that we knew one another.

"Mr. Fox, I don't know who you think I am, but I can assure you, I've never met you before."

Colton looked at me, a glimmer of hurt in his eyes.

"However, it's nice to meet you, and I look forward to helping you with this mess you've gotten yourself into," I said, ripping my eyes from his and sitting down, turning my full attention to the meeting we were about to have. "Mr. Larson, if you'd like to start, I'm tired. I've had an early morning and a long flight, and I'd like to get a move on and go over the details of this arrangement before much longer."

"Sure thing, Miss Cooper. Mr. Fox, if you'd take a seat, we'll get things started so you and Miss Cooper can get acquainted."

I heard Colton mumble something under his breath before he sat down in a chair behind me.

# Chapter Five

Colton

HER REFUSAL TO acknowledge knowing me stung, and it stung badly. Not that I could show it. Not in this room, not with all eyes on me. Perhaps she'd loosen up once I got her alone. After all, she probably didn't want them to know we knew each other either, considering this was her job, so I went along with it. Immediately she snapped her attention back to Larson and spoke to him, completely ignoring me.

I often wondered what had happened to her. She was still beautiful, but the designer suit she now wore and the way she carried herself allowed me to see what she'd become. She definitely wasn't the same girl in that sunflower dress I'd known all those years ago.

The moment she answered Larson, I realized the soft-spoken, kind-hearted girl I used to know was apparently long gone. This woman who replaced her held herself differently. The way she carried herself—back straight, chest puffed out—proved to me she was bitchy and haughty now. Honestly, I couldn't decide if this was good luck, or if my luck really had run out. Of all the PR specialists in the world, it would figure that life would throw me someone from my past. Someone who knew the old me, the one who—dare I say it—walked away from her without another word, but not the man I was now.

Like her, I was far from the boy she remembered, and in my mind, she was just going to be like the others. Someone who didn't understand where I was coming from or what I'd gone through. I was facing the same situation I'd been in the last time.

"Mr. Larson, I'm here to fix Mr. Fox's reputation. That is what I've set out to do, and that is what I will accomplish. I've come up with a plan, and provided that plan is executed properly, then I will accomplish what you are paying me for," Emma said.

It was then that the door opened, and Kent stepped into the office.

"Sorry I'm late," he said, more to me than to anyone else.

"Emma, this is Kent Cole, Colton's agent, the one who hired Image Hackers," Larson said. "Kent, Emma was just saying that she has come up with a plan, but it needs to be executed properly for her to successfully accomplish fixing Colton's reputation."

"I didn't ask for anyone to fix my reputation." I gritted my teeth, glaring at Larson.

I felt Kent place his hand on my shoulder attempting to calm me. "We talked about this," he whispered in my ear.

"Mr. Fox, regardless of whether you asked for help, you need it. You've made a mess of things," Emma said, turning those pretty blue eyes on me. There was a time I would have thought I'd be able to look into those eyes forever, but looking in them now, they were nothing but cold and uncaring.

"Again, like I said, I don't need someone to fix anything. I've done just fine on my own."

She scoffed. "I'm sorry, but a gambling addiction, relationship issues, and beating up a reporter, breaking his arm, isn't what I'd call doing fine on your own."

"What would you call it?" I challenged.

She looked at me with annoyance, as if I should know the answer to this. "Mr. Fox, you call it what you want but let me tell you the truth. Your fans, who, might I remind you, include a lot of impressionable children, whose brains are like sponges and love to mimic their idols, idolize guys like you. Every child I know has someone he or she wants to be like. I'll tell you right now that if this doesn't get fixed, sales of hats, jerseys, and even fucking bobbleheads will stop. Any product with your name on it will stop selling. You'll no longer have promotional contracts, and no matter what team you move to, or play for, the only thing you will be remembered for or associated with will be this one event, not to mention the other things from your past that I've learned about that you think have been buried will all come back to the surface, haunting you forever. Is that the example you want to set?"

"Blah, blah, blah….you sound just like these guys." I huffed, growing even more annoyed because I knew she was right, and that irritated me more than anything.

"Mr. Fox, that's enough. Miss Cooper isn't here to deal with your abuse," Larson said, crossing his arms in front of himself. "She can leave just as quickly as she arrived."

"Let her! I certainly didn't ask for this."

"Mr. Larson, I can assure you I've dealt with many men like Colton Fox. I'm not afraid of him, I won't back down from him, and I certainly won't allow myself to be intimidated by him. If he thinks he'll break me with a few harsh words, he's wrong. He won't. I deal with powerful men every single day, and there hasn't been one yet who could break me," Emma said, looking at Larson and then at me.

I glared at Emma. Was she giving me a challenge, because if so, I'd accept.

"I'll gladly be the first man to break you, sweetheart."

Emma looked at me and glared.

"Fox, I'm not telling you again. You are going to go through this. You will comply with the orders set out by us, and you will fix this situation."

I sat there, looking Larson dead in the eye, not liking the turn of this conversation. I was used to Thompkins telling me what to do, but fucking Larson didn't have a damn clue. He sat behind his desk, and that was about all. He knew absolutely nothing about this life. Then, as if a light switch flipped in my head, a thought floated through my mind that I'd shoved off to the side many times before when I'd been in situations like this. Only this time it sounded better than ever to me.

"What if I retire early?" I said, completely interrupting whatever it was Emma was talking about.

"What?" Kent questioned as the entire room looked at me.

"Seriously, what if I just retire? I can buy a cabin up in the mountains, stay away from everyone. You can all go back to your happy lives, not worrying about what I'll do next, and this will surely make the paparazzi lose interest in me forever."

I glanced over to see Emma looking at me. I wasn't sure if it was my imagination or not, but I was certain I saw a glint of something in her eyes, like she was begging me not to give up on my dream. It was then I realized that perhaps beneath this facade of veneer and ice Emma now had, the girl I once knew might still be in there.

SEVENTEEN YEARS Ago

I WOULD NEVER FORGET the pain in her eyes as I told her I was leaving, at the way her body felt as it shook from the tears she cried as I held her against me for nothing more than a quick moment. I also never thought it would be the last time I laid my hands on her.

My parents had been fighting for years, and I

didn't want that life for myself. Emma and I were inseparable from the first day we met, and in the three years we dated, we never fought. She was my only constant, aside from hockey. Emma and hockey were the only things that took me away from the constant reminder that my parents hated one another.

After I returned from saying goodbye to Emma that night, Dad and I left, driving through the night and the next day to Boston.

Two days later, I pulled my suitcase up onto the bed and pulled out the only two pictures I'd taken from my room back home, placing them on my nightstand. One of them was a photograph of my mom and I and the other was of Emma and me. I lay on my bed and grabbed the frame that contained the picture of Emma and me.

It was a photograph of Emma and me at the summer festival. She had her arms wrapped around me, laughing into my chest at something I'd said, while I kissed her forehead. Fuck, I'd have given anything to see that smile one more time before I left. Instead, I'd left her on her mother's porch, gutted, her beautiful eyes filled with tears.

Emma and I texted daily. She shared with me about school, while I shared with her all about my start on the Junior A team. We often did our homework together via video chat, but as practice and games started, and then I picked up a part-time job, my time became limited.

Months passed after we'd moved. My father didn't like the time I was spending on my cell phone, saying I should use that time for studying or practice, and one morning I woke up to find he'd cut off my plan. Of course I'd told Emma, so she said she'd email or send letters the old-fashioned way instead. Again, weeks passed. We shared a couple of letters back and forth, and then there was nothing.

I sank into a bit of a depression as my parents were still fighting. I'd give my dad the letters to mail from his office, but a response never came. Soon the only joy I had was when I was playing hockey.

When I finally returned home to visit my mother, I did it quietly, not alerting anyone I was coming, including Emma. It was wrong, but I needed that time to visit my mom and to rest. It was the only moment of peace I'd had between games, work, school, and the harsh words my father constantly yelled at me.

One afternoon, before I'd left to head back to Boston, my mom gave me my birthday and Christmas money. She knew I needed a new pair of skates for the upcoming season, so I ventured out to the sports store and tried on a couple of pairs. That was the last time I'd seen Emma.

She was at the mall shopping with Chantal. Immediately, I'd noticed she'd changed the color of her hair, but that was the only difference I spotted. I wanted to go up to her and wrap my arms around her, ask her why I hadn't heard from her, but then I also hadn't been perfect. The last couple of letters I'd written, I hadn't really said anything because I was struggling. My life had become way too complicated. My Dad had turned his abusive words on me, and practices were intense, as was school, so when I had time to myself without my father around, I was completely selfish.

I was already back in Boston on the day of my actual birthday, and I had come in from practice with the mail. I quickly thumbed through the pile, noticing a yellow envelope with my name on it. There was no mistaking who it was from; I'd know the handwriting anywhere. I took what I knew was a birthday card up to my room and had just slipped it into my drawer to read later when my dad stepped into my room.

"Have a good time with your mother?" he questioned.

"Yep, as always."

"Did she give you anything?" he asked, leaning up against the doorframe, looking at me.

I knew what he was asking. He wanted to know whether she'd given me any money. This had become a common occurrence for him.

"Yeah, a few dollars," I said, not really thinking

anything of it until he grabbed my wallet that lay on my nightstand.

Without a word, he flipped it open and reached in, taking the cash.

"What are you—"

"You think hockey is cheap?" he asked, shoving the only money I had deep into his pocket. "I make sure your fees are paid. Your mother pays nothing. So the least you could do is pay me back when she gives you money."

I blinked hard. "Mom gave me that money to go toward a pair of new skates. My old ones are a little too tight and are wearing out. She said she wanted to pay for them to help take some of the burden off."

My father let out a loud laugh. "That's funny as hell. She thinks buying you a pair of skates will help take some of the burden off?"

I looked at my father, making a fist with my left hand, but holding back.

"I need this. I also need your rent money. You are behind. You'll have to get new skates when you get your next paycheck. I've got to go, and make sure you let your girlfriend know to stop sending letters to this house, although judging from the last two letters, I doubt she'll send any more," he muttered.

I frowned as he walked away.

"What are you talking about?" I shouted as I went after him.

"That is for me to know." He turned toward me with an evil grin.

I took a step forward, ready to attack him, but he held his hand out, the look on his face one of anger. "Don't you even think about it. The day you hit me, the day all this ends."

He didn't say another word. He turned and made his way down the stairs and out the front door.

I hated him, everything about him, and if I didn't care so much about my future and wanting out of the hell I was currently living, I'd have gone after him. Instead, I returned to my room, gathered my things, and headed off to the arena where, for a few hours, I could forget everything about myself and this hellish life I was living.

"COLTON! EARTH TO FOX!"

I jumped when I heard my name being yelled and looked up to see Larson staring at me.

"Wake the fuck up!"

"Sorry," I muttered, glancing over at Emma.

It was then I realized that the promise we'd made to one another all those years ago had truly just been a universal lie that everyone tells someone when they are moving away. Perhaps her icy demeanor toward me was because people move, they grow apart, and when you face them again, they are someone you barely recognize, even though they appear to look the same. We were both different people now. No matter how much the other might wish we were the same people as we were back then, we weren't.

"Now, Miss Cooper. Are you okay with staying with Mr. Fox? Meaning, you aren't afraid to be alone with him?" Larson said.

What the fuck was this? I thought to myself. They were acting as if I'd murdered someone when all I'd done was rough someone up a little.

"I am sure I'll be fine. I've dealt with his kind before. I'm a strong woman, and I won't stand for any type of disrespect or any type of out of line behavior from him."

"Well, that is good to know, but please know I will make sure you are protected in the best way possible, so if anything happens and you need anything, you call me," Larson said.

"For fuck's sake, Larson. I'm not deaf, and contrary to what others may think, I'm not a violent man," I bit out, growing annoyed at the fact they were speaking about me as if I weren't in the room."

"Colton, facts are facts. Now, please take Miss Cooper and head back to your place. Help her get settled and make sure she feels at home. Please, also be open to the fact to allow the new you to be underway."

I stood up from the chair I was sitting in and made my way to the door, ignoring looks from both Thompkins and Pamela, and pulled it open. I stepped out into the hall and waited for Emma while she finished up. I wasn't rushing her, but I wanted to get the hell out of here.

# Chapter Six

Emma

TO SAY that the meeting had been intense was an understatement. This was why I oversaw these sorts of projects and didn't take part in them.

I hated the arguing and the resistance from clients who needed the help. Feeling the weight of everything, I stepped out of Larson's office and into the hallway to see a very displeased-looking Colton Fox sitting on a bench across from the door. For a moment, I still couldn't believe I was doing this, but it was true.

He looked at me but said nothing as Kent, Pamela, and Thompkins left, each of them saying their goodbyes, but he said nothing, only watched as they made their way down the hall.

As I watched him, the only thing I could focus on was his demeanor. This man sitting in front of me really was a stranger. He definitely wasn't the Colton I used to know.

"Ready?" I asked, keeping my tone neutral.

"I've been ready for an hour," he muttered as he stood up and made his way down the hall the same way I'd come in. "You are all overreacting to this. I told them to give it time, it would blow over and be gone."

"I can assure you we aren't overreacting," I said, following him down the hall. "If it were going to blow over, it would have by now."

The moment we stepped outside, I saw my bags sitting beside a black pickup truck. Then, as if out of nowhere, the man who'd driven me here appeared and nodded at Colton.

"I have her things. I can put them in your truck, sir," he said to Colton.

Colton looked at me, then nodded. I could tell he was less than pleased to have me stay with him. I wasn't all that excited about it either at this point. Colton led me around his truck, opened the passenger door, offering me a hand as he waited for me to climb in.

"What are you doing? I have arms," I said as he stood there.

"Suit yourself," Colton muttered. "The truck is higher than you'd think. Didn't want you to rip your skirt," he said, his eyes skimming down the length of my body once again.

"Please, I've gotten into plenty of vehicles before—in this very skirt, in fact—and I wear skirts more often than not."

"Again, suit yourself."

This time he didn't wait; he walked to the back of the truck where the other man was loading my bags and began organizing things. I bit my bottom lip as I looked at the foot rail and went to place my foot up onto it, but the pencil skirt I'd chosen for today was too tight and barely had any give at all. I tried it again, this time lifting my skirt a little higher, and placed my heel on the footrail.

As I went to pull myself into the truck, I felt my foot slip, and I screamed as I fell. I tried to grab the handlebars but missed, and that was when I felt a pair of powerful hands grab my waist.

"I got you. Stop fighting me and just relax," his deep voice said. "Let your body relax."

"What the hell are you doing?" I screamed.

"I said relax, stop fighting me."

Against my better judgment, I stopped fighting and

allowed my body to relax against his muscular chest as the scent of his cologne invaded my senses.

"Now, reach up and grab the handrail," he whispered, his warm breath tickling my cheek.

I did as he asked, hoisting myself into the passenger seat, quickly adjusting my skirt while getting comfortable.

"Thanks," I muttered, trying to catch my breath.

"Next time, just take the help, would you?" he bit out, closing my door.

He said nothing as he opened the driver's side door and climbed into the truck. He threw his wallet on the center console and fired up the engine and pulled away from the arena.

I SHIFTED IN THE SEAT, let out a sigh, then reached down and slipped my cell phone into my purse. Once I relaxed in the seat, I glanced over to see Colton watching me.

"What?" I questioned.

"So, are we still pretending we don't know one another?" he asked, glancing at the road and then back at me.

I looked away. When I'd first been told I'd be helping Colton Fox fix his reputation, part of me had been excited, while the rest of me was nervous at the mere thought of seeing him again. It had been years, and while I'd watched him on TV for the first few of his career, it wasn't the same as being in the same room with him.

I remembered what it felt like being in the same room with him when I was younger. He was intoxicating, and from the way my body had immediately reacted upon seeing him again, I knew nothing had changed. Until he spoke.

However, I also couldn't jeopardize my job by allowing others to know that I knew him, or by letting my unresolved feelings for him get in the way. I feared I'd given away the first part the moment he walked into the room and announced we knew one another. It had taken everything in me to compose myself and put on a show, because what I really wanted to do was sit down and talk to him like we used to.

"Well?"

I inhaled deeply and looked out the passenger window.

"We may have known one another a long time ago, but I can assure you I'm not the same girl I once was. So, I'd appreciate it if you'd stop acting like you're outraged at the fact I didn't run into your arms and wrap myself around you."

"I'm not outraged."

"You sure look like you are."

"I'm not. Shocked, maybe, but not outraged. You say it as if we were two people who hung out occasionally, not like two people who once dated and were in love."

"Be shocked all you like. I don't really remember it the way you are describing it," I lied. "You also don't know me. I'm not the dreamy-eyed girl you remember. I've grown up. I'm also in an amazing relationship with a wonderful man, and the only thing I'm here to do is repair the mess you've gotten yourself into. This is my job, so whatever you were hoping to have happen when you got me alone, you can forget it."

Colton chuckled and then shook his head as he looked out at the road in front of him.

"What is so funny?"

"Enlighten me, what was I hoping to have happen?"

"I know guys like you. You think you're all that because of what you do. Think that women will fall at your feet and beg to crawl into your bed at night. It won't happen, so get over yourself."

"Is that so?"

"Yep."

He glared at me as we stopped at a light and then leaned over.

"Newsflash, there, baby girl, I'm not desperate, and you could beg and plead all you want. Nothing will ever happen between us," he whispered, not taking his eyes from mine until I broke contact.

Without looking in the mirror, I already knew that my cheeks were flushed. I sat back in my seat, keeping my back straight. Once we were moving again, I glanced over at Colton. He was no longer looking at me, but watching the road, and that was how he stayed for the duration of the drive.

We'd been in his truck for forty minutes and we hadn't exchanged another word. I was just about to speak when we finally pulled into a quiet little neighborhood in Vancouver. As we drove through it, it reminded me of the area we'd grown up in. Minutes later, we pulled into a driveway, and I stared at the cute little bungalow that was in front of me. It wasn't a place I expected Colton to live in; he struck me as a condo type.

Colton cut the engine and hopped out of the truck without a word to me. I watched in the mirror as he opened the back of his truck and then came to the passenger side door, pulling it open.

"Want help?" he grumbled.

With my jaw clenched, I shook my head no.

He shrugged and muttered, "Suit yourself," and then made his way to the front door while I slid carefully out of his truck.

"Don't forget your stuff in the back," he called from the front door.

Was he seriously not going to help me bring my things inside, I wondered, but when I heard the front door slam shut, I had my answer, especially when he didn't turn around and come back out.

Irritation flooding me, I went to the back of the truck, grabbed my bags, and struggled to get them into the house. I stopped the moment I entered the door. His house was empty. There were a couch and chair, a large-screen TV, a coffee table and two side tables in the front room, but it lacked the things that made a house a home. The walls were bare. The built-in shelving unit was empty. There wasn't even a stack of books! I glanced over at what would be the dining room area. It too was empty.

"Problem?" He questioned, dropping his keys on one of the side tables.

"Nope, if you could kindly show me where I'll be staying, I'd like to get unpacked."

Without a word, he disappeared down the hall, which I could only guess was where the bedrooms were located, so I followed him. He opened one door and stepped to the side.

"You can stay in here," he mumbled, looking displeased.

I looked around the room. Clothing stuck out of the partially open dresser. The bed was messy, showing someone might have napped after they made it. There was a book on the night table, and bottles of cologne on the dresser. Then I noticed a pair of men's boxers lying on one pillow.

"Uh, is this your room?" I questioned, glancing at the hamper in the corner full of dirty laundry.

"Yep. It's the nicer of the two. The other one just has a mattress on the floor and one small lamp. It's basically used when I watch little Mia for Levi and Scarlett, which isn't often, but she loves tents, so I build blanket forts for her and Potato."

"Potato?" I questioned.

"Yeah, her stuffed animal." He chuckled.

Why didn't I insist on a hotel, I thought to myself as I continued to look around. There was no way I was sleeping in here, in his bed, with a pillow his boxers had been on.

"It's fine. I'll take the other room," I muttered.

"This one has an excellent mattress and a private bathroom. The other room, you'll have to use the main hallway bathroom. I think you will be more comfortable here."

"It's fine," I said, still thinking about putting my head on the pillow that held his boxers.

"This room is better suited for you. It even has a small desk that you can work at uninterrupted," he said, walking over, clearing a pile of dirty clothes to reveal a small white desk. He shoved the clothes in the hamper and then came back to the door.

"I told you the other room will be fine!" I shoved past him and went into the hall, to the other bedroom door, and shoved it open. He was right. Just as he'd said, there was nothing more than a mattress and a small lamp on the floor. I walked in, placed my bags over in the corner, then opened the closet door to find a few empty hangers on the rod.

"Suit yourself. Need anything else?" he questioned.

"Nope, nothing," I said, looking around the room, wondering how on earth I was going to make this work. Perhaps I shouldn't have been so stubborn and just used the other room.

I walked over to the door after he'd left and shut it, turned around and walked over to my bags. I began unpacking things, carefully hanging my items in the closet, doubling some shirts and pants along with skirts on some hangers. When I got to my undergarments, I decided to just leave them in the suitcase because I didn't have any other choice, and zipped the lid closed.

I was just about to turn and pull out some of my

toiletries when the door opened and Colton appeared holding a small folding table.

"For the light," he grumbled, leaving it in the doorway.

I quickly grabbed it and placed it beside the mattress, placing the small light on it, and then setting my toiletry bag off to the side. It was then I realized there were no sheets or blankets on the bed, but when I turned back to the door, Colton was gone.

I took a deep breath and then made my way over to the door and poked my head out into the hall. The house was quiet. I made my way down to the kitchen, where I found Colton sitting at the kitchen table drinking a bottle of beer.

"Comfortable?" he questioned.

Comfortable? Was he kidding? I wasn't comfortable. Who lived like this?

"Uh, could I get some sheets?"

"Sorry, baby girl, I don't have any."

I frowned. He'd just told me he made blanket forts.

"Um, you don't have any?" I said again, my voice shaking.

"Nope, that was why I offered you my room, but you insisted on taking the other. So, if you want sheets, you'll have to get some from the store," he said, bringing the bottle of beer to his lips and taking a drink, while looking me directly in the eyes.

I said nothing. I simply turned to leave the kitchen but stopped at the entrance and turned around again, meeting his eyes. "Before I forget, enjoy that beer. It will be your last."

"What?"

"You heard me," I said, heading back down the hall.

"The fuck it is!" he yelled back just as I shut the door to my new room.

As I paced back and forth, listening to the swearing that was going on out in the kitchen, I had a feeling everyone was right. He was going to be my most challenging client yet, and all I could do was look at the four walls of this hellhole he called a bedroom and do my best to keep a level head.

I'D TAKEN a cab to the store and returned with some food, sheets, and a few things I'd need to make my stay a little more comfortable. The first thing I'd noticed was that the driveway was empty, as was the house.

Glad to be alone, I took my time making my room as comfortable as I could. After I washed everything, I made the bed with the new sheets I'd bought, then covered it was the new duvet. I pulled the blinds on the windows and then carried my laptop and notebooks to the kitchen to do some work while I made my dinner.

While dinner was cooking, I made some notes to get the house fully decorated in the coming days. I'd set it out in my plan to have a full-on interview done at the house with The Blue Line Bulletin about the newly rekindled happy couple, and we certainly couldn't have reporters in with the way the house was currently.

I'd just finished eating and had begun working on the article that would be sent out next when I heard the front door open and then the sound of keys dropping onto the table. I looked up and saw Colton standing in the kitchen doorway, scowling.

"What are you doing?" he growled.

"Eating dinner and working on the article for tomorrow, along with your speech for the opening dinner on Friday."

"Tomorrow? What's tomorrow?"

"Well, first, I thought I'd shadow you tomorrow and the next few days. I want to get to know your habits. I know you have practice in the morning, and then we are supposed to have a photoshoot tomorrow afternoon with the team's photographers for the rekindling article. Friday night is the dinner to celebrate the opening of the season. On Saturday, the team is doing a card and jersey signing for…goodness, what was it?"

I said, looking at my notes from the meeting with Larson.

"It's for junior hockey players."

"Yes, that is it," I said, smiling, turning back to my screen.

"What do you have to do with any of those events?"

"I'm here to rebuild your image. So, I'm basically laying out what will happen during those times. I'll be by your side, supporting you as your doting other half at the events and games. We want to put on a show for your fans because right now, as it stands, almost everyone who had been on the list to see you Saturday has backed out, switching to meet one of the other guys."

"Okay, and what were you planning on doing tomorrow?"

"Oh, tomorrow, I'm going to shadow you at practice, and during the day. I need to see how you react in everyday situations."

Colton studied me and then shook his head. "How do you think that having you by my side is going to rebuild my image?"

I tore my eyes from his and let out a sigh as I flipped through my notebook and pulled out the article that in about twelve hours would be published to all sports blogs and apps and handed it to him.

"What is this?" he asked, looking at the sheet and then at me.

"Read it," I said, going back to the sheet I was working on.

I could feel him staring at me, but I wouldn't give him the satisfaction of looking at him. I knew he wanted a confrontation; he'd been begging for it ever since this morning. I began typing away on the keys when I heard him pull the chair out and take a seat.

"What the fuck!" he exclaimed a couple of minutes later, which caused me to look over at him. "What sort of garbage is this?"

"It's not garbage. It's the start of the path to clean up your image."

"I don't know what sort of fantasy you people are living in, but this is just that. It won't work," he said, throwing the page down on the table. "No one is going to believe this garbage."

I got up, grabbed a can of cola from the fridge, and placed it down on the table, then crossed my arms over my chest and glared at him.

"You're wrong."

"Am I? Tell me, who the hell is going to believe that a broken heart is going to be the reason for my actions the night I got arrested. I've never mentioned being in a relationship with anyone, nor is there any photo evidence of me ever being with anyone. In fact, in the last interview I gave, a week before any of this happened, the age-old question was asked once again, and I said I was single."

"Exactly, and that is why the answer you gave couldn't be more perfect. If you actually read the article that was written, you would see that it states the incident with the paparazzi was sparked by questions surrounding 'the end of an unknown secret relationship' that you didn't wish to talk about, but he continued pushing. It states that you were heartbroken over losing the love of your life, and that pushing and prodding tipped you over the ledge you were already standing on," I said, picking up the paper that contained the article, and slipped it back into my notebook.

"Is that what happened?"

"Yes."

"Tell me what happens next in this little fantasy world you're creating?"

"Well, after time apart, the pair of you realized how miserable you were without one another, and you began talking again. One thing led to another, and you both have agreed to give things another try. That is why, tomorrow morning at practice, the photographers will take shots of the two of us inside the arena."

"What the hell for?" he barked.

The article will include those images, and they will also be shared on Puck-Lit-Love.

"The hell they will be!"

"Colton, it's already in the works. Besides, Puck-Lit-Love girlies adore love stories. That will propel your image to change almost immediately, and I know the rest will fall into place from there."

"So, undo it. This story is making me sound like I'm unable to handle an emotional crisis."

"No, it's not. I'm giving your fans and the public a glimpse into the real side of you. A side you've hidden for far too long. The vulnerable side. Besides, everyone loves a love story, and if your fans can be a part of it, they will all swoon, especially the female fans."

"So I've heard," he said, wiping his face with his hand.

"Trust me, this couldn't be more perfect. Your lawyers have told us that there were no recordings from that night, so it's basically your word against his. Since everyone knows what paparazzi can be like when they poke and prod, or at least they should, we are giving you a major out on the public front, while your lawyers are finally taking care of things in private. We want people to feel sorry for you, and while you think it won't work, the fact that you've never mentioned a relationship in public just goes to prove how private and protective you are with that personal side of your life."

"Uh-huh. That is because that side of my personal life doesn't exist. Now, what's your plan for tomorrow?"

"You'll see," I said, sitting down and working on things again.

"I can't wait to see what you come up with," Colton said. "Probably something just as unhinged as this concocted garbage."

"You know, it could be exciting if you just open yourself up to it."

"I highly doubt it, but you do whatever you feel you need to do. Shut the light off before you go to bed."

"I work late, but I'll make sure I shut it off," I murmured, focusing on what I was typing.

I was so focused I didn't see Colton still standing there watching me, and I jumped when he cleared his throat. I looked up at him.

"What?"

"When are we going to talk about this morning?"

I frowned. "What about this morning?" I questioned.

"You know, about your avoidance issues?"

"What avoidance issues?"

"Emma, don't play dumb."

I got up from the chair I was sitting in and went over to the cupboard, grabbing the box of graham crackers I'd bought. I grabbed a sleeve from the box and turned back around but stopped dead. Colton was right in front of me. He was so close I could feel the heat radiating from his body. I could smell his cologne and the sweetness on his breath from the beer he'd been drinking, which I made a mental note once again to reiterate stopping.

He stepped in closer, and I backed up, my lower back hitting the edge of the counter. He was so close I could barely breathe, as he looked me directly in the eyes.

"You going to stand here and pretend you don't remember me?" he said, keeping his voice under control.

"Mr. Fox..." I said, my voice trembling, completely different from the control I had this afternoon.

"Are you going to play it off that you aren't the same person from all those years ago?" His eyes left mine, landed on my lips, and then went back up to my eyes.

I could have sworn someone had sucked all the air from the room, and I jumped when my phone rang. I tore my eyes from his and glanced over at my phone ringing away on the table.

"I, uh, I have to get that," I stammered. "It's probably Mark."

He stood there, his eyes locked with mine, and then

he finally moved back less than an inch, still blocking me.

"Thought you had to get that?" he said, when I didn't move.

I shook as I took a step forward, my body brushing against his as I shoved past him and walked over to the table, grabbed my phone and said hello, my voice trembling.

He chuckled under his breath and shook his head. "That's what I thought."

I listened to Mark start in on what was going to turn out to be a hellish conversation about splitting some assets while I watched as Colton grabbed a cold beer from the fridge. He leaned up against the counter, locked eyes with me and drank down the beer.

The moment I hung up the phone Colton placed the beer bottle on the counter and started walking away.

"What are you doing? What was that supposed to mean? Wait?" I yelled, starting to go after him.

Colton chuckled under his breath while shaking his head, and turned toward me, meeting my eyes. "You'll see," he said, leaving the kitchen once again.

"I thought I got my point across about the beer?" I yelled after him.

Colton turned back around and came right up to me, his body brushing against mine.

"Well, baby girl," he said as he looked down into my face, "your plan starts tomorrow, so my beer drinking will stop then. Have yourself a good night, and tell Mark to tone down the language. A happy relationship doesn't sound like that."

He tore his eyes from mine and took off down the hall, leaving me standing in the kitchen staring after him, just as my cell phone started ringing again.

"How would you know?" I shouted after him, only to hear his door slam shut.

# Chapter Seven

Colton

I KICKED the covers off me and sat on the edge of the bed, running my fingers through my hair. I needed a haircut and made a quick note to get one today while I was out and about. Six had come quickly. I'd listened to her tapping away on the keys of her computer until almost one in the morning, followed by her murmured frustrated voice through the wall our bedrooms shared. Judging from the phone call earlier, I assumed it was this Mark guy, and by the sounds of things, her relationship was far from the perfectly happy status she claimed it had.

I ran my hands through my hair again, yawned,

and then made my way to the shower. Then I got dressed in my usual attire for practice, shoved a change of clothes into my bag for after, and made my way to the kitchen. There was no way she'd be up yet, so I was looking forward to having a quiet breakfast before spending a couple of hours with the boys, only that was quickly pulled out from under me as I rounded the corner.

Emma sat at the kitchen table, already dressed, her computer in front of her, eating a bowl of oatmeal. The moment she noticed me, she smiled.

"Good morning. Hope you are ready to tackle the day," she said cheerily.

I didn't respond. I wasn't a morning person, never had been, and honestly, she shouldn't be especially after being up most of the night. All I wanted was to spend ten minutes drinking my protein shake in peace before I had to train until I felt like I'd be sick.

I went over and opened the cupboard where I kept my protein shake to find that the canister wasn't there. I opened the one next to it and found it wasn't there either.

"Ah, where did my protein go?" I muttered.

"Oh, silly me, I forgot. I hope you don't mind, but I moved it to the cupboard next to the fridge," she sang, her voice grating on my nerves.

I glared at her. She'd been in my home less than

twenty-four hours, and she was already rearranging things.

"Why?"

"Well, it made more sense to move it over there because the blender was under the cupboard, and that way my oatmeal was closer to the stove and the pots."

I took a deep breath and closed the cupboard door, then made my way over to the other cupboard and made myself a shake. I cleaned up my things and was about to head into the living room to sit and drink it down in peace when Emma stood up.

"We should get going."

"We?" I said, clearing my throat.

"Yes, I told you last night. I was coming with you to practice, then I'd be shadowing you for the day."

"You can't be serious?"

"I am. Now, we don't want to be late, and I always enjoy a Cafe Mocha each morning to start my day."

I gripped the cup that held my shake.

"You shouldn't drink that crap."

"Why not?"

"Because it's full of sugar and a lot of other things your body doesn't need."

"Well, thank you for your concern, but it's my body, and I like it, and if we leave now, we should be able to get through the drive-through and make it on time. I've already looked up the drive time, and to make it even easier, I placed an online order that will be ready to be picked up in ten minutes."

"Great," I said, rolling my eyes.

"You should be excited. Today is the start of Operation Fix the Fox," she said, grabbing her bowl and making her way over to the sink.

My eyes washed over her body. I could only imagine what my teammates were going to say when I showed up with her tagging along beside me.

"Operation Fix the Fox?"

"Yep, Fix the Fox. It's the title I gave to this project. Cute right?" she said, crinkling her nose as she stuffed her things into her bag.

"Yeah, really cute. Why on earth would you give this project a title? Let me guess, because you think having a cute title is going to somehow magically help the situation?"

"Cute titles always help. Just relax. I'm only going to shadow you this morning. Like I told you yesterday, I want to note your habits."

"Note my habits?"

"Yep, I want to have you adjust things that perhaps you shouldn't do."

"What, like drink beer?" I questioned, crossing my arms over my chest.

"Yep, exactly like drinking beer. When you drink, you lose the ability to maintain control, and I think that may be one reason you keep getting yourself into these situations."

Out of the pair of us, if anyone knew what drinking did to someone, it was me. I'd not only spent my time dealing with a drunk father when I was younger, but I also watched him drink himself to death in his later years.

"You know what I think?" I questioned.

"What?"

"I think someone in this kitchen needs to mind their own business. I also think she needs to get more sleep at night instead of staying up all hours keeping the person on the other side of the wall awake while arguing with Mr. Perfect."

She didn't even skip a beat; she kept shoving things into her bag and then zipped it closed.

"Well, thank you for that. Oh, and we weren't fighting. Now, instead of worrying about me and my habits, how about we focus on the problem at hand? Now, we need to get going."

I rolled my eyes and then drank down the rest of my shake, half listening to what other garbage she was going on about. The moment she stopped speaking, I rinsed out my cup and grabbed my keys.

"Let's go," I said, leaving her in the kitchen.

I grabbed my bag and headed out the front door, climbed into the truck, and started the engine while watching Emma struggle to lock the door with the key I'd given her. When she finally got into the truck, I began backing it up before she'd even closed her door.

"Wait!" she screamed.

"What?"

I stomped on the brake, causing the door to slam shut, and that was when she turned and looked my way.

"Rule number one: don't kill the love of your life while leaving your driveway," she muttered, her jaw clenched as she quickly fastened her seatbelt.

"Relax there, baby girl. You are far from the love of my life."

I never wanted to laugh so hard as she spun her head around and glared at me.

"Stop calling me that."

"Why? You used to love it once upon a time."

"Well, I don't love it now. So, stop."

"Oh come on, baby girl."

I couldn't help myself when she turned her annoyed eyes my way.

"You know, cute titles always help," I said, mimicking her voice from earlier.

"Just drive."

"I plan on it, and don't worry, I won't forget about your cup of sugar."

WHEN WE ARRIVED at the arena, Emma got out of my truck without a word and headed inside. I'd have thought she'd have waited for me, especially since she wanted to shadow me, but she'd taken off and was nowhere to be found. She could have been in the women's washroom for all I knew because I didn't really look for her either. Instead, I kept my head down and started making my way to the locker room.

I pushed the door open and came face-to-face with my teammates. The room was quiet, and they all sat there looking at me, questions in their eyes.

"What the hell are you all so quiet about?" I questioned, dropping my bag on the bench in front of my locker.

"What the hell is this?" Knox said, standing up, shoving his phone into my face.

I looked down at his screen, seeing the article she'd told me would go out later today had been published an hour ago.

"A phone," I bit back, knowing full well he was talking about the article on his screen.

"Cut the shit. Who's the chick?"

I looked down at the phone, at a photograph of

Emma and I together just outside the back of the arena.

"You've mentioned no one to us. If you were having relationship troubles, you should have told us," Levi said.

That was because there was no one to mention, because this was all fake as fuck, and if there was one thing I hated, it was lying to my teammates. While some would say I'd led them to believe that my bedroom was like a revolving door, that was what they'd assumed, so I just continued to allow them to think that. The last thing I wanted was for Lorelai, Aurora, or the other girls to set me up with someone or for my teammates to think I couldn't get a girl.

"I like my privacy." I shrugged.

"Yeah, but not to mention to us you've been seeing someone seriously for over six years. We're like your brothers, man. You know everything about us."

I just about choked, and grabbed Knox's phone, quickly scanning the article again. When I'd read it the first time, I didn't recall seeing anything about a time-line, but then I'd only skimmed it, but there it was in black and white—six years together.

"I have little to say. I guess, like you guys, I would rather not bring my private life to center stage. Besides, we'd been having issues for a while, long before I got traded, and I really thought we were over, so I figured there was no point in mentioning anything. You know, the whole trade thing and moving to another city, then add in the long-distance thing into an already struggling relationship. It's bound to bring stress into a relationship and to end one quickly," I added, flashing back to when we were younger, seeing her tears when I'd announced I was moving to Boston.

"Well, we wish you had told us, man. Did you mention anything to Lorelai that night? Is that why you wanted her to take you home that night instead of me? She said you were adamant about her taking you. Was it because you wanted a woman to talk to?"

*Thank you, Knox.* There was my out. I grabbed my skates and laid them on the floor, then looked at the boys. "I'm ashamed to admit it, but yeah, that was exactly it. Only I didn't talk with her. That stupid paparazzi appeared out of nowhere."

"Yeah, but it said in the article that they wanted to know more about your breakup. Lorelai didn't mention that to me?" Knox added.

I thought for a moment.

"Well, that is because she didn't hear them. She was already at the door unlocking it when they approached me. I told them to take off, but they followed me to the door where they then accused us of having an affair. I wanted to protect her from the shit we go through, and I guess I just lost my shit." I shrugged.

"You should have told her," Knox said.

"I should have and would have once we were inside. I really wanted her advice," I added.

I did not know where the hell I was coming up with this shit, but it needed to stop. The more I spewed, the deeper into this mess I got, and I didn't even want to be in it to start with. I'd never be able to keep up with this story if I kept going.

"The girls want to know if she is here," Dylan said, sitting down after filling his water bottle.

"If who's here?"

"This mysterious woman." Levi chuckled.

I faced my locker. I didn't want to let them know she was here this morning, but I also knew that they'd figure it out pretty damn quick otherwise when the photographer started taking pictures of us.

"Yeah, she flew in yesterday. She'll be watching practice this morning, but let's not overwhelm her today. Let her get settled in. It's been a lot on both of us, but the moment she is settled, I'll bring her by for everyone to meet her. We should get a move on, boys, or we'll be late otherwise," I said, glancing at the clock, wanting this interrogation to be over.

I gathered my things as the rest of us got ready, and we all headed down to the ice. We all skated around, warming up, but all I could think about was Emma, who I noticed was sitting at the edge of the glass drinking her mocha whatever it was, watching me.

The worst part was, she was still attractive as hell, and this situation right here was one I'd dreamed about. She was all that had been missing during my early career. If the situation were different and she wasn't so wrapped up in herself, I'd take another swing at her.

I took another spin around the ice, and when I stopped and looked over at her, I saw she was talking with one of the newer guys on the team, who hadn't been privy to our locker-room conversation this morning.

While we all skated around, taking turns taking shots on net, I kept my focus on Brad and Emma. Emma was all smiles, laughing at whatever he'd said. Then Thompkins blew a whistle, and Brad skated away from Emma, heading toward center ice.

I tried to keep a focus on practice but knew that Emma was watching me, making notes as she sipped on her drink.

I FELT PUMPED up more than ever, and it wasn't from practice.

To start, I'd hated watching Brad talk to Emma. Watching her smile and laugh at whatever he'd said ate me to my very core. She used to laugh at the things I said just like that when we were younger, and the more I thought about it, the more jealous I became.

I figured she'd have a long list of things I needed to fix after practice and the photoshoot, but she'd not uttered a word when we got in the truck. In fact, she'd said nothing while I chatted it up with the guys after either; she just stood in the background, watching and waiting.

As I pulled the truck up to a light, I glanced over at her, and I watched her for a moment. There was so much tension in this truck that it was making me uncomfortable, but she just sat there staring out the passenger window looking calm.

"If you have something to say, just say it," she muttered without looking at me.

"What?" I questioned.

"There is so much tension in here I can barely stand it," she said, looking over at me. "You were watching me this morning at practice, you kept looking over at me while you were talking with the guys after the photoshoot, and you've been watching me since we left the arena. So, if you have something you want to say, say it."

"No, you've been watching me." I chuckled.

"No, I haven't."

"You have. I even caught you taking photos of me on the ice."

"I didn't. When I wasn't taking notes while you were at practice, I was on my phone trying to find a hotel room for the games next week."

"Why would you do that?" I questioned.

"Well, for starters, I'm not sharing a room with you."

"Why not? What will the media say when they catch us coming out of separate rooms? Did you think of that?"

She didn't look at me; she just shook her head. She was the one who'd thought up this stupid idea, so she should have the answers, but she said nothing.

"I have a room that is big enough for two people, but if you want to make it difficult, make it difficult."

I tapped the edge of the steering wheel with my thumb and then turned to look at her. "What did Brad want?"

"Why? Jealous?" she asked, a soft smile coming to her lips.

"No, I was curious."

"He was trying to get me to wear his jersey," she said, a hint of laughter in her voice.

I cleared my throat and shifted in my seat. "You know what that means, don't you?" I questioned.

Emma didn't answer me right away, and then she shook her head. "No clue."

"It's a statement. Wearing a certain player's number is a statement," I said. "When you are dating a player, you wear his number to every game. It lets people know who you belong to."

"I see, and how many women have worn your number?" she muttered.

"Why? Are you jealous?"

"Please…"

"Honestly, you should wear mine," I added, thinking about all the girls when they attended games. Even little Jackson wore Dylan's number.

"Relax, I'm not a puck bunny," she said, rolling her eyes. "Or whatever they call themselves now."

"Puck bunny works."

"I'm not wearing anything of the sort."

"Well, if you want to make this charade real, you'd wear my number to every event that isn't black tie."

She shook her head and looked at me, and when I met her eyes, she turned and looked out the window again.

"You're serious?"

"Yes, I'm serious. You'll notice that all the other girls wear their guys' numbers at games and at events. Don't be surprised if Aurora, Lorelai, Scarlett, Peyton, and Ella show up to all the events wearing their men's numbers. You'll be the odd one out because you'll be sitting with them in the stands during the game. Fans will automatically think something is up if you're not wearing it, and don't even get me started on what those Puck-Lit-Love girlies will think."

It was like music to my ears, but for the first time since we'd been around one another, Emma laughed.

"What would you know about those Puck-Lit-Love girlies?" she questioned.

"Not a damn thing."

"Well, like I said, I'm no puck bunny. Besides, I'm used to being the odd one out."

I watched as she reached into her purse and picked up her phone, looking at the screen. I caught sight of the name Mark Hart just as she silenced the buzzing and rejected the call, shoving her phone back into her purse.

"Who was that?" I questioned.

"Who was what?"

"Who's Mark Hart?" I asked.

"No one important," she said.

"You're sure?"

She took a deep breath, and then slowly let it out. "If you must know, that is Mark, as in my other half."

"I see. You spoke with him last night, right?"

"That's correct," she said, meeting my eyes before tearing them away from me.

We both grew quiet.

"Do you always argue like that?"

"Who says we are arguing?"

"Well, last I checked, the only time one of my previous girlfriends cried was when we were fighting. Just know that if you need to talk, I'm here, and I don't mind listening."

The tension between us was so thick it made it hard to breathe. She shifted in her seat, clearing her throat.

"Colton, or should I say, Mr. Fox, thank you for your concern, and there may have been a time I'd have taken you up on that offer, but right now isn't the time. I'm here to help you."

"Doesn't mean that if you need to run something past me, I can't help you."

"This is a working relationship only. There will be no personal exchanges," she said, straightening in her seat.

I couldn't help but shake my head. She was seriously acting as if she'd never known me before, and I hated it. Instead of continuing to drive, I pulled my truck over to the side of the road, put it in park, and then turned to look at her.

"So, you get to know all these things about my personal life, but I can't know about yours?"

She looked at me and frowned.

"Well?"

"Correct, because without me knowing the personal side of you, I can't help you."

"Hate to break it to you, sweetheart, but you know shit about me. Oh, and from now on, you'll only ever know what I want you to, and right now, you aren't privy to knowing anything."

"Believe me, I know more about you than you think I do. Oh, and also, I couldn't agree with you more. Truth is, I can barely recognize the person you used to be."

Her words stung. Her words also confirmed where my place was, and it wasn't being her friend.

"There it is, finally, baby girl admits knowing me."

"What is that supposed to mean?" She asked.

"Exactly that." I answered.

"You are impossible," she gritted.

I put the truck back into drive and pulled away from the curb, making my way back into my neighbor-hood. I pulled into the driveway and sat there, waiting for her to get out.

"Aren't you going to shut the truck off?"

"Nope, it's still early, and I have some errands to run," I said.

"Well, I'm supposed to shadow you. So let's go," Emma said, putting her belt back on.

"Not this time," I bit out. "You're staying here."

I could see the shock in her eyes from the tone I'd used, and even though she stared at me, she knew she would not win. She took her seatbelt off, grabbed her purse, and climbed out of the truck. She stood in the driveway watching me as I backed away.

# Chapter Eight

Emma

AFTER COLTON LEFT, I sat in the kitchen, a hot cup of tea in front of me, trying to compose myself. I'd just booked the designer we used to come in while we were away next week to work her magic on the house.

I closed my laptop and wrapped my hands around the warm mug. Perhaps I'd been a little too harsh by not sharing things in my personal life with him, but I was so used to never allowing my personal and business life to cross, it only came naturally. It was a rule I'd lived by, and regardless of who he was, I planned to keep it that way.

I glanced at the clock. It was only six, and I really

needed some fresh air and a neutral space to calm down in. I booked an Uber and figured I'd head downtown and do some shopping. I'd seen a bookstore downtown the other day, and it had been a while since I'd stepped foot into one. I could use a new book to read.

The car dropped me off, and I slipped inside, first grabbing myself a hot chocolate. Then I slowly made my way to the back of the store, where I started browsing the romance section. I was certain the girls at the office would laugh if they knew I read romance books. It had been my best-kept secret to date.

I scanned the section looking for a couple of my favorite authors and grabbed two new releases from the shelves. I continued on, finally taking a seat in one of the oversized armchairs that they had in the store so you could read for a bit.

I took a sip of my drink as I looked out the store's side window. I watched as cars pulled up, dropping off passengers, and then I saw a very familiar black truck with a Dominators logo on the tailgate pull up. As I watched out the window, Colton climbed out of the driver's side and slipped into an unmarked building.

I glanced over to my left to see a woman quietly stocking shelves and waved.

"Yes, Miss, can I help you?"

"I hope so. I have a somewhat odd question."

"Okay." She smiled.

"I was just sitting here, looking out the window, and was wondering if you can tell me what the pink building across the street is? The one without a sign above the door."

"Oh, that's Miranda's Miracle Foundation."

I nodded as I watched Colton come back out, get something from his truck, and slip back inside.

"Oh, I'm not from around here. What do they do there?"

"No problem. My mom went there after she received her cancer diagnosis. There was no way she couldn't afford treatments. When that happens, the hospital directs them to the foundation. They are the ones who help find sponsors for those cases. They put her in touch with a sponsor who could fund her treatment. She told me that a lot of actors and some players from major sports teams sponsor patients."

"That's amazing."

"Some think so. Did you see someone famous go in the doors?" she questioned, glancing out the window. "I always like to watch and see if I can't see someone famous go in."

"Oh no, it just seems like a busy place." I smiled.

"Oh, yes, it is, sadly. My mom actually met Kacey Kabert, you know, the leading actress from the made-for-TV Christmas movie *Christmas Stars* that was such a hit last year."

I did not know what movie she was talking about. I barely had enough time to catch the news most days, but I nodded and smiled anyway.

"My mother told me that while it's great they donate, she's heard that many of the actors and professional sports players are forced into sponsoring as some sort of penance."

"Really?"

"Yes, unfortunately, but just as many if not more do it because they want to do good with their overabundance, or because someone they know or knew went through the same sort of thing, and they hated watching them suffer."

"Wow," I whispered, wondering why Colton was there.

"You know, I think of it often. If it hadn't been for the woman who sponsored my mother, she wouldn't be here today. I really should go over and make a small donation. I know it won't make an enormous difference, but it's what I can offer."

"Never underestimate the power of a donation of any size. You never know who may get the treatment because of the donation you make and thank you for the information."

"You are welcome. Thank you for your kind words.

Is there anything I can help you find?" she asked, glancing at the two titles that sat on the table in front of me. "That's a fantastic read," she said, pointing to one title I'd picked up.

"Oh no, I think I've found what I was looking for. I'm just going to sit back and enjoy the rest of my hot chocolate before I get going," I said, watching as Colton came out of the building, grabbed something else from the passenger-side door, and then went back inside.

"Enjoy your day and your books."

"You too," I said, pulling my phone from my purse.

I quickly searched Colton Fox to see if there was anything in the media to do with Miranda's Miracle Foundation, but nothing came up. There was nothing listed on the Dominator's website either, which told me he wasn't there on behalf of the team. I went to the foundation's website and checked out their public donor page, where I saw many other sports players, along with actors and actresses, but Colton wasn't listed there either.

Why would he keep something like this a secret? If he were in fact helping someone, that would build his image so much more. Something like this might also stop the media from writing the articles they were and focus on all the good he was doing.

I made a note to ask him about this first thing

tomorrow, drank down the rest of my coffee, and headed to the checkout with my books.

FRIDAY

WHILE COLTON WAS in the gym working out at the arena, I had a private meeting with Pamela. I'd gone over how well the event went the night before and how well Colton had handled everything. I wondered if I hadn't been too harsh in thinking he was going to make things impossible for me, because he actually acted better than I'd seen since I'd gotten here.

"The team photographer got some great shots of the two of you at the photoshoot. We did use one of them for the article this morning. I hope that is okay."

"Of course. Could I see them?" I questioned.

Pamela spun her monitor around and showed me some images they'd gotten. When she pointed out the one she'd submitted, it shocked me how much of a genuine couple we appeared to be.

"What do you think?"

"These are great," I said, looking them over again.

"Maybe keep a couple back for another event as well. Oh, and I think we should use these two for the Puck-Lit-Love account," I added.

"Oh yes, I planned to, as well as this one," she said, pointing to one picture where I was looking down at the ground and Colton was watching me while holding my hands in his. The look on his face was so real it looked like he was in love with me.

"That one is amazing," I said. "For sure that one needs to be added to the Puck-Lit-Love account."

"Noted. Now, did you have questions? Is everything going all right? Mr. Larson wants to make sure that everything is fine."

"Everything is fine," I said, hesitating. "I have one question that I'd like to ask."

"Certainly," she said, flipping her monitor back around and putting her full attention on me.

I'd wanted to ask Colton about the Miranda's Miracle Foundation first, but he'd been so closed-off this morning, I decided Pamela would be the better one to ask. Plus, I really wanted to use this in an upcoming article, sooner rather than later.

"Yesterday afternoon, I was over at The Book Nook, and I saw Colton at Miranda's Miracle Foundation. I am wondering if this is something the Dominators support or…"

An odd look came over Pamela's face, and she shifted in her seat.

"That, I'm afraid, is something that you will need to speak directly to Mr. Fox about. I'm afraid I do not have the right to answer that."

"So, you know what or why he is there?"

"Again, that is something you need to take up with him. However, I'm going to suggest to you that you broach the subject with care—and perhaps caution."

"Does that mean you're not going to tell me?" I questioned. "I figured it would be a good thing to get in the papers."

Pamela looked down at her watch and shook her head. "Again, I'd talk to Mr. Fox first before you place any of that information in any article. Now, I'm sorry, but if there aren't any more questions, I'm afraid I am going to have to go. I have another meeting in ten minutes."

I frowned and nodded. "No other questions. I'll be on my way."

I gathered up my things and made my way down to the rink and watched the rest of the team's practice.

FRIDAY

While Colton was gone to get his hair cut for the event tonight, I ran to do some errands. I returned to the house first, put away the things I'd purchased, then sat down at the kitchen table and once again started searching for a room for next week's away games when my phone rang.

"What do you want?" I barked into the phone.

"I just wanted to let you know I will have my lawyer look over your proposal next week."

"Great, the quicker this is all dealt with, the better," I said.

"Oh, would it be okay if I dropped in at the condo? I left something behind that I need."

"I guess," I said, not sure I really wanted him in my place unsupervised. "I can always have Chantal stop in and you can go then."

"I'm not sure I really want her probing eyes there. Bianca will be with me."

I rested my forehead in my hand, feeling my stomach turn. I didn't want her in my space.

"Mark, I hate to break it to you, but I really don't want that piece of work in my private space."

Anger and hurt coursed through my veins. I heard nothing but the sound of my heart beating. I certainly didn't hear the front door open, or Colton throw his keys into the bowl on the table.

"Why not? It's not like we'll be doing it in the bed or anything."

I pinched the bridge of my nose. "I can't believe you'd say that to me."

"I can't believe you either, by the way. Which I thought I'd tell you how much I loved seeing the picture of you and Mr. Fuck-up in the sports section this morning. Looks like the two of you are very comfortable with one another. So, just cut the crap about Bianca, okay."

I knew exactly the picture he was speaking of.

"You two looked at one another like you were together. Shocked the shit out of me, if I'm honest. Perhaps I'm the foolish one of the two of us."

"What's that supposed to mean?"

"Perhaps you used work as an excuse."

Of course, it would look that way to him. I never had the chance to explain what I was really doing with this case because the moment he'd heard about it, he announced we were breaking up. He would have thought I was simply overseeing the project like I always did, not taking part in it.

"Using work as an excuse for what?" I asked.

"To leave. To be with him."

"For the love of…Mark, this is my job. You have no right to say that to me. You announced the end of us the moment I mentioned getting assigned to a case."

"Honestly, Emma, if you'd have stopped giving all your attention to broken men and focused on me, we'd still be together."

Once again, anger flooded my body. I didn't want to hear any more.

"I'll let you know when you can drop by. I don't want her in my space. I mean it. I'm going now," I gritted.

I hung up and threw my phone down on the table and placed my head in my hands. I could feel the tears burn my eyes, but I focused on my breathing, stopping the emotion from taking over. I took one more deep breath, trying to center myself, and jumped when I heard someone clear his throat. I looked up to see Colton leaning in the doorway looking at me.

"My God, you scared the shit out of me," I said.

He looked at me, empathy in his eyes. "Everything alright, baby girl?" he asked, his voice nowhere near as harsh as it normally was.

I hated how he kept probing because I could feel myself breaking down again at his question, but I knew there wasn't any way I could do that in front of him, so I straightened up in my chair and smiled.

"Just a little headache. Otherwise, yes, all is good. We need to be ready at five," I said, turning my attention to the screen in front of me. "You have the address, right?"

He looked at me, concern lining his eyes, but said nothing regarding what he'd asked me. "Yeah, I have it."

"Great, I think I'm going to go get ready," I said, getting up quickly and gathering my things into a pile. "Give my eyes a break from the computer. I'll see you soon."

"Okay, but are you sure you wouldn't rather talk about what's really bothering you?"

"Well, if there was something to talk about, sure, but there is nothing," I said, pushing past him, making my way to my room, shutting the door behind me. I put my things down on the small table, placed the lamp on the floor, and then stepped on my mattress and leaned against the wall as tears slipped down my cheeks.

I could pretend all I wanted things were fine, but they weren't, and I needed to talk about it. The worst part was I knew Colton had always been a great listener. I also knew he had a heart of gold, even if I didn't want to admit it.

I slid down the wall until I was sitting on the mattress and grabbed my phone. I opened up the chat between Chantal and me and sent out our SOS message. Then I wiped the tears away and focused on the job I was sent here to do.

# Chapter Nine

Emma

I'D JUST FINISHED my makeup and checked my phone to see that Chantal hadn't messaged me back yet.

"Ready to go?" I heard Colton call from down the hall.

I stared at myself in the bathroom mirror. I'd decided to wear my favorite dress, and while it wasn't anything fancy, I hoped it would be good enough for the opening event tonight. I really hadn't planned on attending any type of black tie or formal events, so if there were going to be more, I'd have to get some new things.

I smoothed the material out, allowing the deep-green silky material to bunch back up naturally at my midsection, and then swiped on another layer of mascara.

"I'll be right there!" I yelled, then quickly swiped some gloss onto my lips and stepped out into the hallway, sliding my feet into the pair of five-inch black heels I'd left outside the door before making my way down to the living room.

Colton was standing there, looking out the front bay window. The first thing I noticed was that he cleaned up rather well.

While I hadn't noticed it when he'd come home, he'd gotten his hair cut, and while I was getting ready, he'd also given himself a fresh shave, removing the week or two worth of sexy stubble that had covered his cheeks. As I stepped into the living room, I caught a scent of his cologne in the air as I gave him the once-over.

When he turned to look my way, all I could think of was how handsome he looked in the perfectly tailored black suit he wore.

"Ready," I said.

He smiled as his eyes ran over my body. I knew the look; it was one Mark used to have for me years ago. It was also one Colton used to give me when we were younger. It was also a look I'd not seen coming from another man in a long time, and I felt my cheeks heat.

"What?" I questioned as his eyes roamed back over me.

"Wow…you look…."

He stopped again, his eyes washing from my head to my toes and back again for the third time.

"Is something wrong with the dress?" I questioned, panicking that there might be a rip or a stain that I'd not noticed.

"There is nothing wrong with the dress, baby girl. It's just…you look…. stunning," he whispered.

I swallowed hard as my brain realized the words I'd heard him speak, and I slowly lifted my head and met his eyes. Not only were they fixed on me, but they continued to roam my body, taking in every curve I was showing off in this dress. I crossed my arms and cleared my throat.

"Thanks," I said, feeling my cheeks heat. "I, uh, I think we should get going. We don't want to be late."

"You really have a problem with time, don't you?" He chuckled, tearing his eyes from me and grabbing his keys.

"I wouldn't say I have a problem with it." I shrugged.

"It's okay, after you," he said, coming up behind

me, placing his hand on my lower back and guiding me to the door.

"NO FUNNY STUFF TONIGHT."

Those were the first words he'd said to me as we arrived at the event center.

"Pardon?"

"You heard me. Media coverage is going to be everywhere."

He pulled into a parking spot at the far back of the lot and cut the engine.

"Hate to break it to you, but I wasn't planning on any funny stuff," I said, grabbing my small clutch bag.

"Uh-huh," he muttered. "I can already tell you won't be able to keep your hands off me."

"Please." I laughed as he got out of the truck.

He surprised me by coming around the truck and pulling open the door and holding his hand out for me to take.

"Let me help you." I glanced at him, but when he met my eyes, I could see he was serious.

Reluctantly, I slid my hand into his, and he wrapped his other arm around my waist. I placed my other hand on his shoulder as he carefully lowered me to the ground.

"Told you, "He whispered as he winked at me.

"Thank you," I muttered softly, smiling while my hands shook as I took a step back from him so he could shut the door.

"You are welcome."

We walked side by side through the parking lot, and we were just about to round the corner of the building and make our way to the front doors when Colton stopped.

"What is it? Did you want to go over the plan one more time?" I questioned. "Or is it the wording of your speech? If it's that, just give me, I don't know twenty minutes, and I'll fix it."

For the first time since I'd arrived, he actually smiled at me as he shook his head.

"Then what is it?"

"I was just thinking, if we are going to convince people of this lunacy, then we should stop acting as if we are two people who pretend to hate one another and actually start making it appear as if we are dating."

"What do you mean?" I questioned.

"Well, right now, we seem like we are awkward as hell being near one another. We just walked across this parking lot, and if there were anyone out there taking pictures of us, it looks like we just spent the last forty-minute drive arguing."

I thought about what he was saying for a moment and realized he was probably right. It had been so long since Mark and I had shown any type of PDA, I'd thought nothing of it, but Colton was right. Two people who were in love held hands, walked close to one another, and looked happy together.

When I looked at him, I smiled softly. "Oh, I guess you are right."

"I know I am."

He lifted his elbow and waited while I slipped my arm through his, and together we made our way to the front door where he opened it and placed his hand on my lower back while I walked through the doors first. We were greeted and immediately directed to the conference room where the event was being held.

Flashes started going off the moment we entered the room. Colton wrapped his arm around me, pulling me against him, and nudged me.

"Smile for the camera, sweetie," he whispered to me.

As the cameras started flashing, I couldn't help but notice how overwhelming this was. I wrapped my arm around his back as he pulled me close, and we continued smiling for the pictures. I'd occasionally look up at him only to have him smile at me.

Colton thanked the photographers and stepped away the moment other players arrived, taking their spot for photos.

"Wow, I wasn't expecting that. It's overwhelming."

"At first, but you get used to it."

We were one of the first couples to enter the room, aside from Larson, Thompkins, and most of the PR team from the Dominators. We walked over and quietly greeted them, and that was when we heard voices. Stepping away from them, I slid my arm through Colton's.

"Ready for all the introductions?" Colton quietly asked.

"I think so," I whispered, swallowing hard.

Colton kept his arm around me, pulling me against him. "That is Dylan and Aurora. Dylan is our team captain, in case you didn't know, and Aurora is one of our therapists. Right behind them are Knox Evans and his girlfriend Lorelai, another one of our therapists," he whispered in my ear as he lifted his arm, waving at the two couples.

Immediately, I recognized Lorelai from the photographs I'd seen from that night. She looked a little on edge, so I smiled as they made their way over to us, which didn't surprise me, given the circumstances.

"Good to see you, big guy," Dylan said, holding out his hand, which Colton shook.

"You too. Aurora, good to see you, sweetie," Colton said, leaning in and placing a kiss on her cheek. "How's Jackson?"

"He's good. He's with my mom," she said.

"He'll be fine," Dylan said, pressing a kiss to her temple. "She's a little nervous because my dad is also supposed to stop by to see Jackson."

"Mr. Hayes, could we get your picture?" a photographer asked.

Dylan nodded, then took Aurora by the hand, and they went over to where we'd been a few moments ago and had their pictures done.

Colton shook Knox's hand and leaned in and placed a kiss on Lorelai's cheek as well, before greeting Levi, Clay, and Lucas, and then he turned to me just as Aurora and Dylan returned.

"Since we are all together, I'd like for you all to meet Emma Cooper. My much better and way more attractive half."

I could feel him watching me as he introduced me. I smiled and nodded to everyone. Each of them had questions, I could see it, and right now I wasn't sure I could handle them.

"Emma, it's wonderful to meet you," Dylan said.

"Yeah, we were wondering about this mysterious

girl," Aurora said, smiling as she held her hand out for me to shake. It surprised me when I slid my hand into hers and she pulled me in for a hug instead.

"Yeah, the big guy kept quiet about having a significant other, so you can imagine how much of a shock it is to us," Clay added.

"Cut the crap, this is no more shocking than finding out your little sister was impregnated by a teammate. We all, apparently, keep secrets," Knox said, bumping into him.

"Here we go," Dylan muttered, glancing at Colton.

"Yep, here we go," Colton agreed, chuckling.

"Are you still on that, Knox?" Lucas questioned.

"He'll always be on it. I'd have figured finding out Colton had a secret girlfriend would have pulled his attention elsewhere, but I guess I was wrong." Clay chuckled.

"Well, surprise, here she is," Colton said, pulling me against him, pressing a kiss to my cheek.

I could feel the tension in my body as everyone looked at us, particularly Aurora and Lorelai. It was as if they were trying to read the situation, and that was when I realized that the look that was on my face was probably not one of adoration. I'd have to work on that, I thought to myself.

"I'm sorry that we shocked all of you. I'm sure he only kept things on the quiet side because of the move and us trying to figure out the long-distance thing for a while. It's been hard, but we've finally worked things out, and I couldn't be happier to be back here with him," I said, resting my head on his shoulder.

"I'm sure. Long distances can be hell," Clay said. "Peyton and I were long distance until she moved out here. It was tough being away from her when all I wanted to do was be with her."

"Oh, quit putting on a show for the new girl," Knox added once again, punching him in the shoulder.

"It's not a show. It's the truth," Clay added.

"Uh-huh. Secretly he was happy I didn't know, because that way, I couldn't kill him." Knox winked.

Lorelai elbowed Knox in the ribs and then shook her head and stepped in front of Knox and Clay, holding out her hand to me, which I shook as well.

"We are glad you are here, and we look forward to welcoming you with open arms after you complete your move. Well, and before that, of course. Which reminds me, we were talking, and we thought it would be nice to have you both over for a barbecue sometime next week."

I glanced at Colton, who looked at me and nodded.

"That would be lovely," I answered, my mind racing.

"We just thought it would be the easiest way for all

of us to meet you and get to know you instead of trying to get to know you in at one of these silly events, or a game where you can barely hear yourself think."

"For sure." I smiled. "I like that idea. What do you think, sweetie?" I said, turning to Colton.

Colton shifted uncomfortably and then cleared his throat. "Well, why don't we talk about it and see what we can work out after the set of away games this weekend?"

"Guys, he wants to have her all to himself. I can see it. Let's not push," Dylan said, smacking Colton on the arm, which caused Colton to chuckle.

"No, it's not that," I said, placing my free hand on his chest, pulling his attention to me.

"Let's not lie to my teammates, Emma. You know how much I've loved having you to myself, and I recall you saying something similar last night as I was between your legs," he said, leaning in and placing a soft kiss just beside my ear.

Heat flooded my body as I looked at him, the entire room falling away at the same time. What the hell was he doing?

"Looks like we might have some competition, Knox," Dylan said as both the boys laughed.

"Not another one," Aurora said, her and Lorelai giggling.

"Oh, guys, no worries. We don't need to come up

with a date right now. How about we work something out after the games next week?" Lorelai said. "That way, we will know where we stand for the next set of games as well."

"Sounds like a plan. Besides, we should go get our seats. Sponsors are arriving, as is the rest of the team," Dylan said, taking her hand.

"Yeah, let's go," Knox added, taking hold of Lorelai's hand and leading her away from us as well.

The moment they were all gone, I turned to Colton. "What was that?" I quietly asked.

"What was what?"

"That comment?"

"Oh, you know, just playing it up," he said, winking at me. "Let's go find our seats."

ONCE WE FOUND OUR TABLE, I took a seat while Colton made his way over to the bar to get us a couple of drinks. While he was gone, I opened up my notes to see that he was the only player seated at this table of sponsors and other media journalists.

I was so nervous that, before I read the speech I'd written for Colton, I checked to see if Chantal had responded, but there was nothing there but a few messages from Mark, which I ignored.

I'd shut the screen of my phone off just as Colton placed a glass down in front of me and slid in beside me.

"What's that?" I questioned, nodding toward the glass.

"Gin and soda."

"Is that what you have?" I questioned, praying that it wasn't as I nodded toward the glass of clear fluid with a lemon.

"I have water," he said, meeting my eyes.

"Um, I'm not sure why you chose this as a drink for me."

"Because you look like you could use at least one to take the edge off. So, drink up," he said, placing his hand on my upper thigh before standing to greet some of his sponsors, who were taking their seats at our table.

I thought about what he said for a moment. Did I look nervous, I wondered, or that haggard? What would one drink hurt? I picked up the glass and took a sip as I felt my phone vibrate on the table. A quick look at my phone showed me another set of messages from Mark, which, while Colton continued to greet people, I quickly skimmed the previous messages along with the current one and responded. Then I drank down my glass and stood while Colton introduced me.

"I'll be back in a moment," I said, whispering in his ear.

"Where are you going?" he questioned.

"To the bar." I smiled. "Do you mind watching my phone?"

"Not at all, but do you need another one already?"

I nodded. After seeing the messages Mark had left about dropping in to the condo and his need or want to meet up with me soon, I definitely needed another.

"No need."

He lifted his hand in the air and in a moment a server appeared. I ordered another drink and then asked to be excused.

"Where are you going?"

"To the ladies room. Please watch my phone," I whispered.

"Sure thing, sweetie."

As I walked away, I glanced behind me to see that he had turned his attention back to the table.

As the night went on, things seemed to go great. So far, Colton was perfect in every sense, which I was thankful for as it made my job so much easier, especially after my third drink.

Every once in a while, Larson or Pamela would glance over in my direction, and all I'd do was smile and nod, letting them know things were going fine, when in reality I'd been so buried in my phone or my glass that I really didn't have a clue if things were going well or not.

After dinner, the speeches started, and before I knew what was happening, Colton stood. The crowd was silent as he reached down and gently tapped me on the arm. I'd forgotten I was supposed to go up on stage with him while he gave his public apology.

"Are you coming?" he whispered.

I swallowed hard, then stood up, smiling at the people sitting around the table while placing my clutch and phone down. We walked hand-in-hand to the side of the stage, then he paused, waiting for me to climb the stairs first, which I did carefully. As I took the first few steps, I quickly remembered why I didn't drink.

Colton approached the podium while I sort of stopped and stepped off to the side, but when he looked over his shoulder at me, I remembered telling him I'd be right beside him during the entire thing.

I took a step forward, making my way over to him, taking hold of his hand as he held it out for me to take. Then he turned to the crowd.

"Ladies and gentlemen, Mr. Colton Fox," the emcee said, stepping off to the side.

Colton stepped up to the podium while I stayed beside him.

"Good evening. I'd like to take this opportunity to first say thank you to Guy Larson, Coach Thompkins, to the assistant coaches, my teammates, and to all the sponsors for being here this evening. As you all know, each year we take a night to welcome in the coming year, we celebrate our successes, we honor those of us who have decided to retire, and those who played an exemplary game the year prior.

"However, this year, there is something else that we are doing. An apology. During the end of last season, I was dealing with some personal issues, after having recently ended things with the love of my life of six years. I'd been partying it up after the last winning game of the first round of playoffs and needed a ride home. Lorelai Anderson was the one who drove me home, and once we arrived, a reporter cornered me outside of my home. They began pressing the issue about my breakup. If anyone knows me, I keep these personal matters to myself, but somehow they'd found out.

"As they continued to press with the questions they soon started in on Miss Anderson. The next thing I knew, I was being thrown in the back of a police car. Articles were printed, rumors started, charges are pending. I'm sure you're all wondering why I am here tonight.

"First, I'd like to apologize to my teammates for

leaving them during the most important part of the year. It was because of me, the stress I caused to my brothers, and the absence from the games that made us miss the cup. I'd also like to apologize to the owner of the Dominators, Guy Larson, a man who has given me another shot at redeeming myself. Thank you for your patience and guidance. I'd also like to apologize to my fans. I'm sorry I let you down. It won't happen again.

"Now on to the next announcement. I'm happy to say that after many hours of conversation, the love of my life has decided that we deserve another chance, and I am happy to introduce you to her tonight."

I looked out at the crowd and lifted my hand in a small wave, really wishing I'd never agreed to getting up on this stage as I noted all the cameras that were flashing in the crowd.

"I also want to say how excited and lucky I am to be with the Dominators for another season, and this year, we won't let you down. All the way to the winning goal, boys! Now, enjoy the rest of the evening, and we will be happy to answer any questions anyone might have tonight."

Colton nodded to the emcee, and then with his arm around my waist, he guided me over to the side of the stage we'd come up. The moment we were back down off the stage, I grabbed his hand.

"I'm just going to slip into the ladies room."

"Sure, is everything alright?" he questioned.

I nodded. "Just need a moment," I said, leaving him and heading right for the ladies room.

The moment the door to the stall closed, I took a deep breath in and slowly exhaled. I'd never imagined being up there in front of all those people would be as overwhelming as it was. I'd also never imagined how the speech I'd written him would affect me, or how he'd look at me when he said the love of his life.

I'd almost cried right there.

I'd never known what had happened between us for things to end the way they had. I'd also not given it very much thought until we were up on that stage and I'd listened to him speak those words. It didn't matter if he meant them or not; it just affected me for some reason.

I ripped off a square of toilet paper and dabbed my eyes, then I flushed, opened the stall door, and stepped out, meeting Aurora face-to-face.

"Emma? Are you okay?" she asked, concern filling her voice.

God, did I seriously look like I'd been crying?

"Yeah, I'm fine. I don't know what came over me. When I came off that stage, suddenly I wasn't feeling very well."

"Oh, yeah, stage fright. You'll get over it."

"I hope so. It was very overwhelming up there."

"Let me go and get my purse. My doctor gave me something to help with that. It's nothing serious but should help you take the edge off."

"Oh, no need. I've just taken something. I was hoping it would kick in soon," I said, rubbing my stomach.

She gave me an odd look. "Where's your purse?" she asked.

I felt a wave of heat wash over me. "Oh, I left it at the table with Colton. I took the tablet right before his speech."

She nodded. "Okay, I'll see you out there," she said, giving me a curious look.

"See you out there," I said, washing my hands.

"Hope you feel better," she said and then left the bathroom.

Moments later, I returned to the table and listened to the rest of the speeches while sitting beside Colton.

# Chapter Ten

Emma - Saturday Morning

AFTER WE RETURNED HOME from dinner last night. I'd made myself a cup of tea after Colton retired to his room and carried it to my room and curled up in bed and read for a while. It didn't take me long to drift off.

I'd woken before Colton and was sitting surfing through social media when he appeared in the kitchen doorway.

"Morning," I sang.

"Is it?" he said, running his hand over his face.

"It is. I was just doing some work for tonight's benefit dinner."

"Great," he mumbled, going over to the cupboard.

Ignoring him, I put my focus back on my social media, swiping to the next post, and just as he started the blender, he appeared on my screen. I couldn't hear what it said at all, but I saw myself off to the side. It was a video from the event last night.

At the exact moment the blender stopped was when I raised the volume on my phone, the sound almost deafening me.

"What the hell, would you turn that shit down," Colton barked.

Immediately, I stood up and looked at him, a smile on my face.

"What?" he said, rolling his eyes.

"You're probably not going to believe it but look!" I said, shoving my phone at him.

He glanced at the screen and shrugged his shoulders, not showing an ounce of excitement. "So what? I see myself in these stupid clips all the time. If you're excited because you saw yourself, you'll get used to it and it will annoy the hell out of you just as it does me."

I rolled my eyes and let out a huff. "It has nothing to do with me. It has all to do with the five million views this has gotten since last night. Colton, people are happy for you."

"What for?"

"Look, just look at the comments. You are Puck-Lit-Loves' new favorite."

"Great," he muttered, drinking down the rest of the shake.

"It is great. This is what we wanted. If they reacted this way to your speech last night, just wait until they get our interviews."

"Awesome, well, while you do whatever it is you are doing for tonight, I have to pick up my suit for tonight. So, have fun, and I'll see you later."

I watched as he rinsed his shake cup out then he left the kitchen. I frowned, then looked down at the screen, smiling to myself. It was working. So far, my plan was working.

I'D GONE OVER many things for tonight's benefit dinner, including where we were seated and with whom. There were a few donors that Pamela had warned me about, but she assured me that none of them were being seated with our table.

We'd arrived at the hotel the benefit was being hosted at, spoke with the other players, and once guests started arriving, we all made out way to our tables. Once again, Colton grabbed me a couple drinks at the bar, and once again, I broke my own rule about drinking while he had water.

Things seemed to be going well, and so far, once again, Colton was perfect in every sense, following my exact directions, which I was thankful for as it made my job so much easier, especially when I was on drink number three.

With dinner finished, and conversation pouring I was surprised when another couple approached out table, placing their hands on the back of the two empty seats at our table.

"Mind if I join you, Fox?" a man questioned, a woman who I assumed was his wife stood beside him.

Immediately, Colton shifted, and an uncomfortable look came over his face. "Ah, sure thing," he said, sitting back down beside me after shaking hands with him.

I leaned over to him once he'd sat down. "Who is that?"

"John Martins," Colton whispered.

I grabbed my phone, quickly pulling up the list of donors Pamela had warned me about, and sure enough there was his name. Since I knew this could turn bad, I placed my hand on Colton's upper thigh and leaned into him once more.

"Just remember, keep things in check, okay. Just like we went over," I whispered.

Colton nodded, picking up his glass and taking a drink.

I took a drink and then noticed John was watching us. I gave him a small smile, but he looked away and whispered something to his wife.

"So, Colton, I saw your apology last night," John said, the entire table turning their focus on him.

"Great, what did you think?" Colton asked.

"Well, let me see, I think that most of it was great, but I don't believe a fucking word of it when it comes to the two of you."

I was mid-swallow when he'd finished, and I couldn't help but begin to cough.

"Why is that?" Colton asked.

"Oh, I don't know. The two of you don't really seem to mesh."

I sat forward in my seat, about to say something to John, when Colton placed his hand on my upper thigh.

"It's okay, sweetheart," Colton said, stopping me before I could say anything.

I grabbed my phone and was about to message Pamela to see if we could get John relocated to another table when I noticed Mark had messaged me. Instead, of closing the message like I should have I quickly got lost in a replay of a conversation we'd already had, quickly forgetting all about asking Pamela to move John and his wife. In fact, I was so deeply rooted in the conversation that I also forgot that I was supposed to be focused on the now until I heard voices raise.

"It's not okay. It's rude!" John yelled.

I lifted my head from my screen to see he was glaring at Colton and then me. I had no idea what he meant by that, but I noticed the entire table was now looking my way.

"Unfortunately, it may come across as rude, but Emma is a very busy executive and sometimes her career takes precedence," Colton said, looking over at me.

Just as John was about to say something, my phone vibrated against the tabletop once again, this time going off more than once.

"For the love of god," John said, throwing his napkin down.

Immediately, his wife gripped his arm, quietly reminding him where he was, when Colton turned to me.

"Get up from the table, deal with whatever it is, and get back here," he said, gripping my upper leg tightly, his eyes burning with frustration.

I didn't say a word, but I did as he suggested, and as I walked away from the table, I heard Colton continue to apologize on my behalf.

I'd just made it into the ladies room in time for my

phone to ring. I quickly looked under each stall to make sure I was alone and then answered.

Mark's harsh and hurtful words hit my ears, quickly sending me to tears as he brought up another article he'd seen that had just been published, along with the video from last night that had gone viral. This was why I never drank, because whenever I did, I lost the ability to have a backbone, and I allowed my emotions to take over. I struggled to compose myself before someone came into the bathroom.

I'd had no clue how long I'd been in the bathroom, but when Mark finally ended the call with the date in which he'd planned to return my key, I hung up the phone, dried my eyes, and then stepped out of the stall to an empty bathroom.

I shut my phone off and made my way back over to the table. Immediately, I noticed John and his wife's empty chairs. Then I noticed Aurora was with Colton, helping him with receiving donations from the others.

"Where is everyone?" I asked, looking around the empty room.

"They left." Colton shrugged.

I glanced at Aurora to see a worried and concerned look on her face.

"What do you mean, they left?"

"The event is over. They served dessert while you

were in the washroom and did the final presentation, donations have been collected, and everyone left."

How long had I been in there?

"Did you achieve your fundraising goal?" I questioned, looking at my watch, shocked to see the time.

"Nope."

I felt my stomach sink.

"Why not?" I asked, swallowing hard.

Colton cleared his throat and looked from me to Aurora, giving her what I could only perceive as a warning glance. I could tell there was something else he wasn't telling me, and I was about to ask her what had gone on when Larson approached the three of us. Aurora quickly thanked Larson for the evening and then excused herself and made her way across the room to where Dylan was waiting to leave with the rest of the guys. Once they had made their way out of the room, I grabbed my clutch from the chair and went to thank Larson as well before we left, but he spoke before I had the chance to.

"Well, Colton, how much did you raise?"

Colton glanced at me, and then shrugged.

"What do you mean?" Larson said, mimicking the shrug.

"If you're asking if I hit my goal, I didn't."

Larson looked over at me with a disapproving

glance and then back to Colton. "How much are you short?"

"Forty thousand," Colton added.

"I gave you the smallest goal. How the hell did you not hit it?"

"Look, I'm sorry, but why did you seat Martins at this table? You know my past with him."

"I know your past, but we are supposed to be fixing that, and I didn't seat him with you." Larson said, turning his attention to me.

"Don't blame her. You know better."

"Colton, I'm warning you."

"No, I'm warning you. As usual, Martins pissed me off. He got into my face earlier this evening with his underhanded comments, hitting me below the belt. Then he started in on Emma, and once she'd left the table, he continued questioning me about my personal issues. I warned him not to bring it up, but he didn't stop. So, when he didn't heed my warning, that is when he got what he deserved," Colton said, crossing his arms over his impressive chest.

Panic filled me. I didn't know what happened after I'd left, but before I had, the only thing he'd said was that he questioned our relationship.

"What do you mean he got what he deserved?" I questioned, gripping his forearm.

When he didn't answer me right away, I looked at Larson, who now had his eyes trained on me.

"Where the hell were you? Perhaps you were a mistake. Maybe I should fire you and cut his contract on the spot."

"Mr. Larson, I'd like to draw your attention to the videos from last night."

Larson said nothing, only shook his head and looked at Colton.

I felt like I'd completely failed as I looked at Colton, wondering what had happened once I'd left. I could only imagine, since he was right—the man had done nothing but antagonize him when I'd been present. He hadn't been nice to me either, and there were a few times I was going to step in and say something, but Colton appeared to have it under control. I guess I'd been wrong.

I swallowed hard and straightened my back, digging deep inside myself. I already felt like a bus had hit me after my conversation with Mark. I had one hell of a headache, and I truly wasn't in the mood for this shit, but I sucked it up.

"Mr. Larson, I apologize. As you've seen, I'm normally much more attentive and on point than I was tonight. I can assure you I am taking this task seriously and will strive to do better. I will contest that Colton isn't lying. Mr. Martins was incredibly rude most of the evening, and I was going to step in at one point and have Pamela reassign his seat, but Colton seemed to have things under control. Apparently, something must have happened on my last bathroom trip, and for that I'm sorry I wasn't here to support him. So, to prove to you just how serious I am about fixing Mr. Fox's career, I'll cover the outstanding donation tonight, so he isn't short on his goal."

I knew I had more than enough in my emergency budget from the firm and that if it meant saving face for Kerry and Image Hackers, I'd do anything. I'd just pay back the account over time from each paycheck.

Without waiting for another word, I sat down and dug into my purse, feeling around for my corporate checkbook, when I heard Larson clear his throat.

"Miss Cooper, thank you, but that won't be necessary. My apologies."

"Yeah, Emma, no need. I'll cover it," Colton added, placing his hand on my shoulder. "I really should make a donation. It will help with everything."

I looked at both of them and shook my head. "No, I insist," I said, not taking no for an answer, and wrote out a check, signing and dating it, handing it to Larson.

COLTON DIDN'T SAY a word the entire way home, and neither did I. We both exited the truck, and I waited while he unlocked the front door. He surprised me when he held the door open, waiting for me to enter the house instead of barging in first like he usually did. He placed his keys on the small table against the wall, like always, and kicked his shoes off.

I slipped my heels off, then sat down on the couch. I wasn't used to wearing such high heels, and after two nights of wearing them, my feet were killing me. I rubbed my right foot, letting a soft moan escape as I dug my fingers into my foot.

"Sorry about tonight."

"Don't be. It was my fault."

"No, it wasn't. I'll repay you," Colton muttered as he took his suit jacket off and laid it over the back of the chair before sitting down beside me on the couch.

"Don't worry about it. I think you did the best you could tonight, given the circumstances. Not that you didn't try."

"How would you know?" he questioned, tapping my leg.

"What?" I questioned, looking at him.

"Give me your foot," he said.

I shook my head.

"Give me your foot," he insisted, locking eyes with me.

When I knew he would not let up, I shifted in my seat, straightened my leg, and placed my foot in his lap. His large hands wrapped around my foot, enveloping it. He then dug his fingers into my foot, hitting all the right spots with just the right amount of pressure, resulting in a tingling sensation that moved through my body.

"So how would you know?" he questioned again.

"How would I know what?" I murmured, opening my eyes.

God, his hands felt amazing, better than anything I'd ever felt, and he was only rubbing my feet.

"How would you know I did the best I could tonight?"

"What is that supposed to mean?" I frowned.

"Well, to be honest, it appeared that you had your focus on something else tonight. I could have been an absolute asshole to each one of those people, and you'd never know the difference."

"Yes, I would."

"Right, between Mark and his harassing ways and your trip to the bathroom, it was like you weren't even there. What's going on between the two of you?"

He sat there, rubbing my foot, waiting for me to answer him as if he were entitled to know everything that was going on in my personal life, which I'd already made it very clear he had no right to know anything about. When I didn't answer him, he stopped working my foot, placed his elbows on his knees, and leaned forward.

"You don't deserve to be treated the way he is treating you."

"How do you know how he is treating me?" I questioned.

"Well, I read one of his messages over your shoulder, but I also heard how he spoke to you on the phone that first night."

"What?" I gasped.

"I didn't look on purpose. I came over to you with a drink and saw it."

I couldn't get angry. It wasn't like he'd gone snooping.

We both grew quiet. As much as I didn't want to lean on someone, I knew I needed to, and while maybe he wasn't the smartest choice, he was here. I was about to say something when I felt Colton's hand on my leg, this time his touch tender, unlike earlier. I looked down at his hand and then over at him.

I could already feel the tears building as we sat there staring at one another.

"Dammit," I muttered under my breath. "Don't cry, don't cry, don't cry."

I blew out a shaky breath as a tear finally slipped down my cheek.

"You're probably going to hate me even more than you already do, but I lied to you when I first arrived." I sniffled.

"About?"

"My happy relationship," I said, lifting my eyes to his.

"Well, I may just be some dumb hockey player in your eyes, but I do know what a happy relationship sounds like, and I hate to break it to you but—"

"You don't need to. I already know. We split about three weeks ago, right when I got assigned to your case."

"And you want him back?" Colton asked quietly.

I shrugged. "When I think about all the good times we shared, yes, of course, I want them back. I'd love to have my happily ever after. However, with Mark, sadly the bad times outweigh all the good."

I did not know why I was telling him this. I'd never even told Chantal these things. It had to be the alcohol. Then it was as if something released inside of me and the tears fell, my entire body shaking as I sat there, my face in my hands, and cried.

I felt him shift on the couch, moving closer, pulling

me against him. When the tears finally stopped and I lifted my head, I felt him place his fingers under my chin, lifting my head so he could look me in the eye.

"Emma, if all you can remember are the bad times, and you must search for the good, then it's not worth it. I've heard his voice through the phone, the things he says… You don't deserve to be treated that way."

"He didn't always treat me like that," I whispered.

The moment I stopped speaking, he leaned forward and placed his mouth on mine. The moment our lips touched, I closed my eyes and felt my body weaken, the same way it used to when we were younger. The moment he pulled away, all I wanted was to feel his lips on mine again.

"He should never treat you the way. You'd see the difference if you were mine. I'd treat you like gold."

He leaned forward and kissed me again, and when I felt him rub his thumb against my cheek, I opened my eyes. I had to look away from those glass-blue eyes, because if I continued to look into them, I'd be his forever, and I wasn't here to be his. I was here to help him fix things.

"I know, but I'm not yours," I whispered. "We tried that once upon a time."

The moment the words left my mouth, and I saw the look in his eyes, I wanted to take them back. I hadn't said them for any other reason than to remind myself that we weren't together.

I brought my hand to his cheek, leaning in and bringing my lips to his one last time. When I broke away from him, his eyes lingered on me.

"We have an early morning, so I think I'm going to go to bed," I said.

I got up from where I was sitting, leaving him in the dark, and began making my way down the hall, trying to figure out what had just happened. It was as if I wanted the punishment of tasting him one last time. I was halfway down the hall when I heard him clear his throat.

"Emma?"

"Yeah?"

"Did you get yourself a room for next week?"

I stopped in my tracks and closed my eyes as panic and worry filled me as my mind spun. I could feel my heart beating hard in my chest, not only from the kiss we'd just shared but from the reminder I didn't have a room.

"No," I said, my voice cracking.

"What are you going to do? Where are you going to stay?" his deep voice asked.

I turned around and looked at him now standing in the room, a bit of light coming through the window from the streetlight cast him in a bit of light. It took me by surprise how handsome he looked in the dark room, the way the light came in through the large front window and hit his eyes. The stream of light stressed some of his best features, and I realized that the tingling sensation that had washed through me when he'd kissed me had more to do with how attracted I still was to him than anything else. I swallowed hard.

"I guess you are going to have a roommate, if you'll have me. You told me you had plenty of room."

He didn't move; he said nothing; he just sat there staring at me as I stared back.

"Good night, Colton," I said.

It took everything in me to tear my eyes from him and make my way down the hall where I opened the door to my room when I heard his voice.

"Night, Emma."

# Chapter Eleven

Colton

I WALKED into The Sushi Garden and immediately saw Dylan raise his hand and wave. They were seated toward the back of the restaurant, so I made my way to the back to find Knox, Lucas, Clay, and Levi all sitting around the table as well.

"Hey, guys," I said, slipping into the booth, noticing we weren't at our usual table. "Why the change in booths?" I questioned.

"Well, we weren't sure if you were bringing Emma," Dylan added. "You two have been inseparable since she returned."

I'd expected Emma to be awake when I got up this

morning, just as she'd been every morning since she'd arrived, only this morning her bedroom door was closed, and when I pressed my ear to it, I heard nothing. I didn't wake her; instead, I felt a sense of relief that she would not be at my side today.

"Nah, she was still asleep when I left this morning. So, I figured I'd leave her to it."

"Tire her out, did you, big guy?" Levi said, smacking me on the shoulder.

I couldn't help but chuckle. The only one of us who was tired out was me. After we'd shared that kiss last night, I'd barely been able to sleep because I couldn't stop thinking about how it had felt. I also couldn't get the look I'd seen in her eyes out of my head when I'd told her she deserved better. I could tell she didn't think she deserved someone better.

"Nah, she's just been exhausted," I said, feeling a little on edge as the guys all looked at me.

This was the first time I didn't allow them to expand on the idea they'd suggested. Normally, I'd just run with it, but not today, not about Emma.

During the entire practice, everyone seemed indifferent toward me. It was almost as if they knew something but weren't sure how to bring it up.

"So, is everyone ready for the away games?" I asked.

"Game on!" Lucas replied, then the table fell silent again.

I looked at each one of them, noticing they each had the same questioning look on their faces.

"What is it?" I asked.

"Alright, fine, if none of you idiots want to bring it up, I will," Knox said, clearing his throat.

All the guys shifted in their seats and dropped their eyes to the menu in front of them, except for me and Knox. We just sat there and stared at one another.

"What the hell is up with this Emma chick?"

"What do you mean, what the hell is up with her?" I questioned, trying hard to maintain composure and remember what I'd said in the locker room the first day she was here.

"Yeah, man, we just want to know the truth, because something is off," Dylan added.

"There isn't anything off. You all should know what it feels like to rekindle with someone."

"We do, that's the problem…" Levi added.

"What is?" I questioned.

"Well, we watched the two of you and the night of the opening dinner, things were fine, but then last night, while you two put on a good show, something wasn't right," Clay added.

"Yeah, it's almost like you've put her up to this or something," Dylan added. "I heard Aurora talking to

Lorelai in the back of the truck last night on the way home and something she'd said to me didn't sit well."

"What did she say?" I questioned, praying that she'd done as I asked.

"She mentioned to Lorelai that she doesn't think you two are legitimate."

"What?"

I could feel my heart racing. While Larson hadn't told me to keep it from my teammates, I'd decided to because I figured the less they knew, the better it would be.

"Yeah, so we had Lucas do some digging," Dylan added.

I glanced across the table at Lucas, who kept his head down. That was right; he was guilty as fuck if he couldn't bring himself to look at me.

"You did what?"

"I told them, Colton, but they made me do it. I said that maybe things were awkward because you felt awkward not mentioning Emma when you arrived."

"Stop kissing ass and tell him what you found out," Knox added, elbowing Lucas.

"Fuck, I'm so dead if Larson finds out. I sleep with his fucking daughter, you know," Lucas added. "He could come into the house at any time and chop my fucking dick off."

Normally, we'd all laugh at a comment like that,

but the table was deathly silent because you could actually see the fear in his eyes.

"What did you find out?" I questioned.

The look I got from my teammates told me all I needed to know. I took a deep breath and looked at the table in front of me.

"Well, since you all know the truth, there isn't much that needs to be said. Larson hired her. Well, my agent did. After everything that went down at the end of the season, you all know I was put on a fucking leash. This is part of that leash."

"Seriously?" Dylan asked.

"Seriously. Only she isn't a stranger to me."

Knox looked at me as the rest of them did, unsure what to make of what I'd just said.

"How do you know her?" Lucas asked.

"We go back to high school."

"Wow, I'm shocked," Levi muttered. "Here I thought you were just keeping quiet about things and working through them."

Knox shook his head and looked over at me. "Were you two an item?"

I nodded. "For a good four years, until my senior year at high school when my parents split. We tried our hand at a long-distance relationship."

"What happened?" Levi questioned.

"It was my dad. He was a bastard. The only good

thing he ever did for me was pay for my hockey, until he wouldn't even do that. Anyway, he cut my phone shortly after I got on with the Junior A team in Boston. When I'd told Emma, we decided to write letters the old-fashioned way, but my dad, man, he never gave me a single one of her letters. I found them all after he died, shoved in a shoebox in his closet. Her last letter was dated exactly two years after I'd moved, saying her goodbyes. Until she walked through that office door last week, I hadn't thought of her in years."

"Kind of like Scarlett and I," Levi added.

"I guess." I shrugged.

"Any chance you might think of getting with her for real?" Levi added.

"We saw how you looked at her. It's not like the entire thing is fake," Dylan said, meeting my eyes.

He was right. The entire thing wasn't fake, and I'd meant what I'd said to her last night if she were mine, if I could only have another chance at her, she'd be treated like gold and I'd never let her go.

"Nah, she's not ready for anything. She's just gotten out of a relationship. She made the message quite clear to me last night."

"That means nothing. The least you could do is try," Dylan added.

"Yeah, man, give it a shot."

"I don't know.'

"Did she come right out and say no?"

"Well, no, but—"

"But what?" Clay questioned. "Are you going to sit back and watch her get away a second time?"

"Yeah, tell us now, do you want her or not?" Dylan added.

"God, I haven't a clue," I replied. "Did you immediately know you wanted Aurora?"

"Oh, here we go," Knox muttered.

"Did I know if I wanted her? Considering I lost my appetite for every other woman on the planet after we'd shared that one night together, you're damn right. There was never a question in my mind, and when I got her back, I was damn well relentless. She was going to be mine, and I would not stop until I had her."

I thought about what he said, then to when I'd seen Emma again for the first time again, and then back to last night. I still couldn't forget that kiss and how sweet she'd tasted.

"Yeah, man, even though Lorelai and I started out rocky, god I can't even imagine where I'd be had I let her walk," Knox added.

I nodded, thinking about every one of her letters. I'd read them all after I'd found them in my father's closet. I thought about her words, telling me about the tears she'd cried when I never responded, and then her words telling me that she'd decided it was time to move on. I'd read those letters often, frequently pulling them out when I was feeling sad or lonely, especially after my mother had passed. Her letters, her words, had gotten me through that difficult time, because next to my mother, Emma had been the closest woman to me.

"Okay, well, I have no clue on how to go about winning her back." I sighed.

"Well, we could always get Lorelai, Aurora, and Peyton…" Knox began.

"No, no way, no women. This stays between us."

"No worries, we are at your side, man. We will help you!"

"Yeah, we will open up a new chat and you can dump all your issues into it. The advice will be stellar."

"Yeah, I'm sure. I've seen all the advice you guys share," I said, chuckling.

"Let's eat. I'm starved," Lucas said, focusing on his menu.

"Yeah, food first, plan next," Knox said. "I can't think on an empty stomach."

"Well, we also need to go over the game plan for the next week, so fuel up." Clay chuckled.

"Which game plan? The game's game plan or Colton's game plan?" Levi questioned.

"Both!" Dylan said, raising his glass and clinking it against mine.

As everyone looked at their menus, I took a quick

moment to look around the table. I'd never really thought about it before, but these guys all brought me into the group without a second thought. They'd treated me like family from the start, when no one else had. I'd truly found my home here with them. Now I just needed to focus on getting the other part of home I wanted.

FOR WHATEVER REASON after lunch with the guys Sunday morning, I spent the entire night in my room after telling Emma I hadn't been feeling well. She'd looked at me with a worried expression, mentioning something to me about looking over design plans for the house.

I had no idea what she was talking about, so I ignored her, said good night, and made my way down to my room.

The next morning, neither of said anything on the flight. She did some work and then read the rest of the flight, while I watched a movie.

When we arrived at the hotel, she sat in the lobby while I got in line to check in with the rest of the team, then we made our way to the room. The moment I'd opened the door and she followed me in, I heard her gasp.

I'd expected that reaction, so I ignored her and threw my bag down on the bed, and that was when I heard her mutter something under her breath.

"Is there a problem?"

"What do you mean, is there a problem? Of course, there is a problem. There is only a king-sized bed in here," she said, throwing her phone down onto the desk and placing her laptop bag on the chair.

"Sorry there, baby girl, I hate to break it to you, but this is a standing reservation when we come into town, and I normally stay alone. I also prefer room when I sleep."

"Yeah, but you're not alone this time."

I couldn't help but chuckle to myself as I looked at her, seeing the flush on her cheeks as she looked at the bed and then around the room.

"Maybe the couch is a pull out," she said, running to check.

"Nope, not a pull-out, and this hotel doesn't provide cots. So I guess that means you're sleeping next to me."

"Colton, we uh, we can't share a bed," she said, looking at me.

"Why not? Whose bright idea was this? Certainly not mine. I offered to retire, remember?"

"It wasn't mine either."

"Well, I'm going to beg to differ on that. Guess you should have continued your search for your own room because I'm sure that would have given the media something else to talk about."

She turned away from me and opened her bag, carefully pulling out the neat piles of folded clothing and placing them in the top dresser drawer. I just shook my head, watching her, and opened my bag, pulling out handfuls of unfolded clothing and shoving them into the other drawer. When I finished, I zipped up the bag and turned around. She stood there in front of me, her mouth open and an appalled look on her face.

"What?" I questioned.

"Nothing."

"No, baby girl, it is something."

"I told you, stop calling me that, and it's nothing."

"You're irritated because of the way I pack, aren't you?" I asked, knowing full well it was exactly that.

She turned her back on me, pulling out her perfectly piled undergarments and placing them beside her clothing. "I just cannot understand how you can be like that."

"Be like what?"

"Look at your drawer, now look at mine."

"So?"

"What do you mean, so? It's like you're twelve. Everything is in a heap. Your clothes are a wrinkled mess."

"I like things wrinkled. It helps with my unkempt appearance."

"You're ridiculous."

"You may think I'm ridiculous, but it's how I like things," I said, throwing my bag to the floor and laying down on the bed.

I watched as Emma shook her head and continued to unpack her things while muttering under her breath.

"If you have something to say, it would be better if you actually said it out loud. I mean, I don't want to pry, but obviously you have a problem with me, baby girl."

"No problem," she said, grabbing her toiletry bag and heading for the bathroom. I flipped the TV on and began searching for the sports channel. She came walking out of the bathroom and went right over to the coffeemaker, quickly ripping open one pouch of coffee and shoving it into the small machine, then opening a bottle of water and dumping it in the back. Then she plugged it in and waited for it to brew.

I was focused on watching some highlights from the games the team had played last week when I caught movement out of the corner of my eye. I glanced over and saw Emma looking a little flustered as she looked around, went to run toward the bathroom, but stopped and started mumbling, "oh no," more to herself than to me.

"Problem?" I questioned.

"Oh god, oh god, please stop," she cried, now fiddling with the button on the coffeemaker.

As I watched her in a panic, I saw something start to drip off the tabletop and onto the floor and knew immediately the coffeemaker was leaking. I'd dealt with these stupid two-cup hotel room coffeemakers enough to know they never worked properly unless the stars aligned. I ran into the bathroom, grabbed two towels, and then ran back into the room, gently pushing her out of the way.

"Oh my God, I've never seen…here, let me…" she said, trying to step in front of me.

"I've got it," I said, pulling the plug from the wall to stop the flow of coffee, and dropped the towels down on the tabletop, soaking up the coffee.

"Colton, please, I got it," she insisted, trying to grab the towel to help me.

Look, please, you've done enough," I barked, soaking up the coffee with the towels. "If you want to be helpful, get me another towel."

With her head down, she went into the bathroom and returned with another white towel, holding it out for me to take, which I dropped onto the floor and stepped on it, soaking the coffee that had spilled onto the rug.

The moment I was finished, I took the soiled towel and placed it in the bathroom on the floor and then came out to find Emma sitting at the small table, her face in her hands.

"I'm so sorry," she cried.

Ignoring her, I walked over to the phone, called room service, and asked for a carafe of coffee to be sent to the room, then I requested some more towels. When I hung up the phone and turned around, she sat there looking at me with tears in her eyes.

"That is why you order coffee from room service. Those stupid little two-cup machines never work," I barked, a little more harshly than I'd intended.

"I said I was sorry."

"Being sorry has nothing to do with it. Knowing better does."

She mumbled under her breath again and looked up at me, fire in her eyes. "You're the same!" she yelled, causing me to take a step back.

"What are you talking about?" I questioned, frowning as she continued to glare at me.

The silence in the room was almost deafening. Then her phone vibrated against the table, and it was that moment I realized who had been messaging her every single time I'd seen her on her phone this morning. It was the only reason I could think of for her eruption a few moments ago.

His harassing ways weren't doing her any good, and I'd had enough of it. She knew she was worth far more than that.

I walked over and picked up her phone and brought it over to her. She looked up at me with a questioning look.

"Open the message and tell him to stop messaging you," I said through clenched teeth.

"Who do you think you are?" she said, crossing her arms in front of her chest. "Telling me what to do."

"Emma, it doesn't take a genius to figure out this guy is ruining you. This is fucking Heidi Pendalton all over again!" I yelled.

Emma looked like she'd seen a ghost and the shock that lined her eyes almost scared me.

I paused, not knowing where that had fucking come from. I hadn't thought of Heidi Pendalton in years, or the exact moment I'd met Emma, but as I looked at her, it all came flooding back.

"You remember that?" she gasped.

I said nothing. Instead, I made my way over to the door and pulled it open.

"Where are you going?" she questioned quietly this time and with no anger in her voice.

I needed to get out of this room. I needed a moment to breathe, to focus.

"I forgot, but I have to meet the team at the arena," I answered, looking back at her to see her grabbing her purse. "Whoa, where do you think you are going?"

"With you."

"No way, you are going to stay here and get this shit with him under control. The team isn't paying you to be bullied by your ex-boyfriend. They are paying you to fix my issues, and that, baby girl, is exactly what you are going to do. Sit down, figure your shit out, and get to work. Your coffee should be here within the hour."

I opened the door to the room and pulled it shut behind me, leaving her standing in the middle of the room, and made my way down to the lobby.

IT WAS after eleven when the team returned to the hotel. I was going to join Dylan and Knox for some drinks but then remembered my stupid drinking ban, so I said good night and made my way up to the room.

I had hoped Emma would be asleep by now, but

when I opened the door, the lights were on, as was the TV, and Emma sat at the small table, papers scattered all over the place.

"Don't you ever sleep?" I questioned, really not in the mood to talk to her right now.

"I told you, I work late."

"Well, since you're working late, did you tell that jackoff to back off?" I questioned.

"I'm not answering that, and as for working late, I do most of my best stuff at night."

"I bet you do," I muttered, grabbing my boxers from the drawer and heading to the bathroom.

"What is that supposed to mean?"

"Not a thing," I muttered.

"Wait, don't you want to see the article I wrote?" she said, just as I got to the bathroom door.

I stopped, stood still, and glanced at her over my shoulder.

"Baby girl, it's almost midnight. What I wanted was to have a couple of drinks with the boys and come up here to silence, crawl into bed, maybe watch a little porn, jerk off, and go to sleep."

I wanted to laugh at the disgusted look as it washed over her face.

"Ugh, seriously?"

"Yes, seriously. Don't you dare tell me you don't rub one out occasionally. To be honest, you should probably do it a little more often than you do. You're so uptight. It would probably help with that and ease a lot of the stress you are carrying," I said, looking her right in the eyes.

"You know, being a difficult ass isn't a personality trait," she said, getting up and shoving a piece of paper into my chest.

Her eyes met mine, and I couldn't help but smile as I took in the look of disgust on her face once again. I honestly loved getting under her skin because I knew that the woman she portrayed wasn't the one she was. The only glimpse I'd seen of the girl I'd once known was that night in my living room, the night we'd kissed.

"Read it."

She shoved me out of the way and shut the bathroom door. I glanced down at the paper she'd given me, reading the first few lines, but I immediately stopped when I noticed the mention of the cancer foundation.

How the hell did she know about this? Only a handful of the guys, Pamela and Kent knew about the foundation named after my mother. I stared at the words, all of them blurring together. I could barely tear my eyes from the sheet of paper as she walked back into the room.

"Well, what are your thoughts? I think the interview and photoshoot at the house when we return and the things in the article will really help things. I mean, think about what the Puck-Lit-Love girlies will say when they find out the hockey hero has a soft spot for cancer patients."

"This isn't going out. In fact, it's never going to see the light of day, so I don't care what the Puck-Lit-Love girlies are going to think," I barked, ripping the paper into pieces, sprinkling them onto the floor.

She crossed her arms in front of her, and I watched her chest rise and fall as she looked at me.

"That's mature, rip it up. Do you honestly think I don't have another copy?"

"Have as many copies as you want. If you publish that article—"

"If I publish the article, what?" she asked, crossing her arms in front of her. "I'm sure you want things to get better for you, so I'll leave?"

I turned away from her, dropping the boxers I'd held in my hands down on the bed.

"What did I do?" she questioned. "I'm simply showing them a side of you—"

I whipped around to find her right behind me. She looked up at me, and I looked down at her.

"Listen, I'm telling you, that is not to be printed. I mean it."

"I don't understand. If you'd just allow this side of you—"

"If I'd just allow this side of me what?"

"If you'd just allow people to see the real you—"

"Look, I won't tell you this again. You can do your best to fix this situation for me, but I'm going to ask you to stay out of my personal private life and keep your mouth closed when it comes to it. Got it?"

"But, Colton, you don't get it—"

"No, you don't get it. I'm in the light enough. People don't need to know every time I take a fucking breath. They don't need to know about my personal struggles."

I had no clue what had come over me, but as I stood there looking down into her face, I saw fear in her eyes for the very first time, and that look said it all. Maybe she was right. Maybe I was just like him, and if that were the case, that meant I was just like my father, because this anger, this attitude I had, was exactly how my father would have reacted.

I slowly backed up, making room between us, and then I grabbed my wallet and my keys.

"Colton, please stay and talk to me. I don't understand," she said, taking a step toward me.

"No, Emma," I said, shaking my head.

"Where are you going to go?"

"I just think that maybe we need some space. Have a good night."

I pulled the door open and allowed it to slam shut

and made my way to the elevator. I didn't care what she thought or what her rules were. There was no way in hell I wanted any of that information getting out, nor did I care if she didn't want me drinking. I was going to wind down and enjoy my brothers' company, and I knew for a fact that the beer was going to go down well tonight.

## Chapter Twelve

Emma

I SAT in the dimly lit room working away on organizing the upcoming interview with *The Blue Line Bulletin* and had also spent time working out the details for the in-home interview with *Off-Ice Affairs*, the newest and hottest magazine publication in the hockey world.

When I was finished sending off the final email asking for the interview date for the in-home interview, I filled my mug with the last of the tea I'd ordered and sat down on the edge of the bed.

I grabbed my phone, flipping through every article I could find about Colton Fox, because I couldn't help but wonder why he'd kept telling me that people didn't need to know about his personal struggles, but no matter how much I read, or how many years I went back, there was nothing more than the mention of the gambling, which in my eyes wasn't really as bad as they'd made it out to be. I'd seen many other sports stars in worse situations than that.

It was close to two by the time I decided to shut everything down and crawl into bed. I'd hoped that Colton would have been back before now so we could have had a conversation, but he wasn't.

I got ready for bed, crawled in and had just drifted off when I heard Knox and Dylan giving Colton shit outside the door. I lay there staring up at the ceiling, listening to him swear and then laugh.

"Shhhhh…" he said, laughing as he pushed the door open.

"Get your ass to bed," Dylan whispered, pulling the door closed.

"Yeah, go get her, big guy." Knox chuckled.

"He isn't going to get anything in the shape he's in." Dylan laughed.

I glanced over to see him walk into the room, then struggling to get his shoes off before he fell into the dresser. Both the guys laughed while Colton swore under his breath. The guys shut the door while Colton made his way into the bathroom, where he shut the door.

I closed my eyes and took a deep breath and jumped when I heard something in the bathroom crash to the floor, followed by Colton muttering a string of curse words. I had half a mind to get up out of bed and say something but decided against it. We'd been through enough tonight, and it was probably better not to confront him in the state he was in. Instead, I rolled over and faced the wall.

I MUST HAVE FALLEN asleep before he came out of the bathroom because when I opened my eyes I was surprised to see it was a few minutes past six.

Kicking the covers off, I sat up and glanced over my shoulder, expecting to find Colton beside me, but the bed was empty. I frowned, stood up, and made my way to have a shower when I saw him face down on the small sofa in the room. His legs hung over the arm of the sofa and his head was contorted at an odd angle. I could only imagine how uncomfortable he must have been.

"Rise and shine," I said, standing beside him, my arms crossed in front of me.

I reached down and poked him hard in the chest.

"Huh, what?" he asked, opening his eyes but then shielding them with his hand as the light hit them. "What…what time is it?"

"It's time to get up. We have a photoshoot and interview with a sports influencer from *The Blue Line Bulletin* in twenty minutes.

I wasn't sure if I had allowed him to sleep so long because I felt like getting back at him for breaking my rules about drinking or if I was just completely pissed off at life right now. I figured it was a bit of both, and I poked him in the chest again, this time noticing it was like poking a rock. He covered his eyes with his arm and grumbled something under his breath.

I didn't move; I stood over him, waiting for him to get up.

"I have practice," he muttered. "No time for an interview."

I huffed and shook my head. "Practice was four hours ago," I sang.

Colton bolted into a sitting position, glancing around the room to find the clock. I tried not to laugh; I'd never seen the man move so fast.

"Are you serious? I missed practice?"

"Yep. Your phone has been going off since six -thirty."

"You've been awake all this time?"

"Yep, I figured you needed your sleep. After all, you were out late last night partying it up."

"Yeah, but if you knew I had practice, and you knew the team was trying to get hold of me, why didn't you just give me a nudge?"

"Why on earth would I do that?" I questioned looking him directly in the eyes.

"Why would you do that?" he mimicked. "Why the fuck wouldn't you?"

"Well, for starters, you are a grown adult who shouldn't require a babysitter. Yet here we are. I recall asking you not to be out drinking—it's bad for your image—but you have clearly not taken that as a serious task, given the situation we are facing right now. Second…oh gosh, what was the second? Oh, yes…that is right, I am only doing what you asked of me."

Colton looked at me, his face screwed up in confusion. "Well?" he barked.

"Give me a minute. I am just trying to remember how you explained to me."

I brought my finger to my lips and looked up to the ceiling, pretending to think. "Oh yes, stay out of your way and keep my mouth closed," I replied, turning and sitting down behind my computer, checking the direction to our interview.

"You've got to be fucking kidding me," Colton barked under his breath, getting up off the couch and grabbing his jeans and shirt off the floor.

"Oh no, I'm not kidding because, unlike you, I do as I'm asked."

"Do you? Does that mean you messaged him like I told you to?" he asked, getting up off the couch.

"Is my phone still going off?" I questioned.

When he looked at me, I swore I could see an apology in his eyes, but I didn't wait for it. I turned around and started gathering up some papers, shoving them into my bag.

"You should go get yourself ready. Like I said, we have to leave in ten minutes."

"COLTON, it's great to have you here to talk hockey with us. However, your fans already know your talent.

"That they do."

"The other night, at this season's opening dinner, you got up and made a very public apology to not only the team but to your fans, and you introduced us to Emma."

"That is correct."

Colton hadn't seemed to relax since we'd gotten to the interview, and he looked even more stressed now, so I reached over and interlaced my hand with his.

"Then came the night of the benefit, and there have been some reports of one of the donors who you've had some issues with in the past actually questioned your relationship with Emma."

"That's correct," Colton said, clearing his throat.

"Can you explain to us what happened?"

I felt Colton shift in his chair, taking my hand and holding it with his opposite hand and placing his arm around me where I could feel him rub my back. This was his chance to clear the situation, and he was looking directly at me instead of answering.

"Well, I think we will let Emma take this one," he replied.

This interview had been going on for the better part of half an hour. When I'd set it up, I was told it wouldn't last longer than ten or twenty minutes. I glanced at Colton, hoping he'd get the hint and answer instead, but all he did was wink at me. He had answered every question up to this point. Granted, I'd given him the answers since my friend who'd arranged the interview had given me the question list prior. It had made it easy, but this question—this one hadn't been on the list.

I shifted, then smiled.

"Of course, darling, I'd be happy to," I said. "I can't speak on behalf of the donor. All I can say was that perhaps he'd have been better off being seated at another player's table. It's not unknown that he has never been a fan of Colton's, and he'd been rather difficult from the start of the night. Colton dealt professionally with the entire situation. I could tell he wasn't thrilled when he left, and he did so without donating, but you can't win them all."

"That is so true, Emma."

"Now, the fans are dying to know, as are we. How are things between the two of you now."

Again, Colton shifted in his seat and looked at me, giving me a gentle nod.

I smiled. "Things honestly couldn't be better. This man right here…is the only one for me. It was torture being apart from him, and I'm just glad that we could work through the tough spots and come back to one another," I finished, meeting his eyes.

Colton met my eyes and looked into them. As I looked back, I noticed he was staring so intently at me it made me feel uncomfortable. We were both so focused on the other that neither of us heard the next question.

"Sorry to interrupt, got to love watching two people in love." The interviewer chuckled. "Colton, does that mean the hockey world may see a proposal coming soon?"

Once again, Colton shifted in his seat, as did I this time. While my friend wasn't the one doing the interview, she'd assured me they would stick to the questions she'd given me. However, these questions weren't ones that were on the list. Since I'd arranged this without Pamela, there wasn't anything we could do aside from answer.

"You don't need to give us the date or anything, or how you'd propose. We just want an answer to a question the fans have been dying to know. You've been so private with not only your personal life but also about your relationship, they just want a hint of things to come, as does the Puck-Lit-Love world. Would you be able to give us a brief insight?"

I looked over at Colton, prepared to answer, and that was when he looked at me. Instead of answering the question, the moment his eyes connected with mine, I leaned forward and pressed my lips to his.

Heat and shock flooded my body as I realized what I had done. I was just about to push him away when I remembered where we were, but the sounds of cameras constantly clicking and gasps from those in the audience invaded my thoughts. Before I could even accept what was going on, his tongue slipped between my lips and washed through my mouth.

I felt his arm wrap around me, pulling me closer, and he tapped my right elbow with his finger. I brought my right hand to his cheek. I closed my eyes, allowing his kiss to take me over. Then my brain caught up with my actions and where we were, and I broke the kiss.

"Colton, answer the man's question," I murmured, glancing up to see nothing but a sea of cameras, which meant that the photographers I'd arranged weren't the only one's present.

"Well, Colton?"

"When I get around to it, that is when it will happen," he answered, looking me directly in the eyes.

*What kind of answer was that?*

"When he gets around to it, that's when it will happen. Emma, what are your thoughts?"

I cleared my throat and said the only thing that came to my mind. "To me, it never matters if he ever proposes. Like I said, as long as he is mine and mine forever, that is all that matters to me."

As we stared at one another, the room broke out in applause, and the cameras kept snapping pictures and somehow my lips ended up pressed against Colton's once more.

WHEN THE INTERVIEW ENDED, we stayed for a few more pictures, but once that finished, we were free to return to the hotel and get ready for the game tonight. Colton had gotten a call just as we'd left the interview that the team was meeting prior to the game tonight to go over some plays.

I'd hoped he'd just get ready for his game and forget what had gone on at the interview, but the moment we'd returned to the hotel and were safely behind the locked door of our room, Colton grabbed hold of my hand and stopped me from walking away.

"What the fuck was that?"

"I don't know. My friend at the magazine provided me with the questions. I answered them for you, and… somehow the interviewer added in his own questions."

"That isn't what I'm talking about."

I froze. I knew what he was talking about—the same thing I'd been thinking all the way back to the hotel after the interview. The same thing I'd been thinking ever since he'd kissed me first the other night.

"What are you talking about?" I questioned, hoping that if I played dumb, he'd just let up on the subject.

"The kiss, Emma, what the fuck was that?"

My cheeks heated, as did the rest of my body. I needed to get out of here. I could still feel his lips against mine, and everything in me wanted to feel them again.

"I don't know. Why don't you ask yourself that? You kissed me back! In fact, you kissed me first!"

"That I did, in the privacy of my home, not in front of all the cameras and reporters. I certainly didn't start it this time."

"We don't have time to talk about this. You have a game to get to," I said, trying to get out of the situation.

"Oh no, we have plenty of time," he said, his voice deepening.

I glanced at my watch and shook my head.

"Well, we can either discuss it, or perhaps we should just recreate that kiss and find out exactly what was going through your mind when you leaned in and kiss me in front of the cameras."

I stood there, afraid to move. I wanted to feel his lips against mine so badly I could taste it. He was watching me, staring at me, almost willing me to step into him. Instead of giving him not only what he wanted, but I wanted as well, I spun around, opened the door, and took off down the hall to the stairwell. I sped off down the stairs, praying he wouldn't follow me.

I TOOK comfort in the sounds of nature as I walked through the enormous park down the road from where we were staying. When I came to a park bench, I took a seat and looked out over a large pond where children were feeding ducks and smiled to myself. Then, I pulled my phone from my pocket and opened the chain of messages between me and Chantal. She still hadn't responded to my message that I'd sent a few days ago.

Emma: Got time for a quick chat?

I hit send and then placed my phone on my lap and sat there listening to the sounds of the birds. Within seconds, my phone vibrated against the bench.

Chantal: My goodness, I'm so sorry I didn't see your message from last week; things have been chaotic.

Emma: No worries.

Chantal: Emma, it was our SOS message, which means you really needed me. How are things going with the sexy hockey player?

Emma: Got an hour?

Chantal: Oh dear.

Emma: Okay well maybe two.

Chantal: What's going on?

Emma: What isn't going on?

Emma: First, Mark thinks I used this case to leave him for Colton. He has been so unfair to me over the past few days, horrible actually, what you would call downright abusive.

Chantal: Uh huh. So, even though you are legitimately working for Image Hackers, Mark thinks it's all a lie.

Emma: Yes, but only because this time I had to get my hands dirty. In case you haven't seen the news, I'm in a ton of articles and pictures with Colton, which Mark thinks are legit.

Chantal: So the facade is working, which is a good thing then. God, I love your life. You're like a secret agent, so mysterious.

Emma: Yeah, I'm a secret agent who's falling apart.

Chantal: Look, these insecurities this man has was going to be the downfall of your relationship anyway. No successful happy, and I stress happy, relationship would have one of the couples being this way. It's not a bad thing you two are no longer together. This is a good thing Emma. Now, tell me, how is it going with Colton?

Emma: Well, I decided not to allow our past to co-mingle with this project, and I was staying focused on the task at hand. It was going fine, until....

Chantal: Until what?

Emma: Until the other night, and then again this morning

Emma: I broke down after one of the events and told him about my breakup. I needed someone to talk to, and he just happened to be there when I was on the cusp of a breakdown. He kissed me, and then I kissed him, only he kissed me in the privacy of his own home, I kissed him during this morning's interview I'd set up which means there are legitimate images of us kissing that will be all over the media.

Chantal: YOU WHAT?

Chantal: *running to check socials*

Emma: Oh god, no, don't do that, I haven't even looked yet. GAHHHHH

Emma: I know, I shouldn't have, and I have no idea what I was thinking when I did it, but I did and...

Chantal: What happened during the kiss this morning?

Emma: *whispers* He kissed me back

Chantal: eeeepppp ....and

Emma: I was afraid you were going to ask me that.

Chantal: Well?

Emma: It was amazing. The worst part is that it was amazing in front of all kinds of people, but it was the same amazing as it had been behind closed doors.

Chantal: Do you think this could lead to something more?

Emma: It was a kiss...okay two kisses, and while they were wonderful...

I tapped the edge of my phone, trying to figure out what I wanted to say, when my phone pinged.

Chantal: I think you should find out.

Emma: Oh god no.

Chantal: Why not?

Emma: Because I'm not that person anymore

Chantal: Bullshit, until you met Mark, out of all the guys you dated, all you did was talk about what a loss Colton Fox was when you'd break up with them, and how you wished you could have a second chance.

Emma: Chantal, I did not.

Chantal: You did. Please do yourself this one favor and stop lying to yourself. Perhaps this is life's way of giving you both a second chance.

Emma: You have no clue what you're talking about. Colton would never be interested in a girl like me.

Chantal: Why not? He kissed you didn't he?

I STARED AT HER MESSAGE, and then my phone rang, scaring me to pieces. I quickly answered, "Hello."

"HE KISSED YOU, DIDN'T HE?"

"He kissed me out of pity, because I'd been crying."

"Woman you are impossible. This is it, Em, this is the chance you've been waiting for."

"You make it sound as if I've been holding my breath, waiting for another chance with Colton Fox."

"Uh, not in the literal sense, but subconsciously you have."

"Now who is the impossible one."

"Emma, I love you like a sister. You may not have come directly out and said it, but I'm the one who has been listening to you for years. Throughout college and most of our twenties, all you ever did was watch his games for a glimpse of him. You tracked the teams he played for, waiting for trade announcements when you knew he might be moving."

"So what?? I like hockey."

"You like hockey? Really, the only time you ever watched was on the nights he played."

"So, I liked his team."

"Right, Emma, again, babe, I love you, but a hockey fan who loves the Predators, is a fan of the team regardless of the players who play on it. They don't switch being the fan of a team because a player leaves. Sure, they may still enjoy watching them when their team plays against the team they moved to, but they don't change teams."

"What are you saying?" I questioned, afraid that what she was going to say was something I'd only thought to myself.

"Go after him, say goodbye to the fake life you're

living, and say hello to finding the real you again, with the man you've wanted forever."

"Yeah, but what about working things out with the relationship I just lost? Don't you think that is worth a try?"

"Emma, I'm going to be very honest with you here. I never liked Mark from the day I met him. My best friend changed when she met him and turned into a person who few people liked. I stuck around only because I knew the real you, not the fake one you portrayed, and when we got together and Mark was gone, you were the real you. The message when it popped up on my screen tonight was from the real you, the one Colton brought out in you, the one I miss dearly."

"Chantal…"

"If being around him for a week has changed you this much, I'm going to go out on a limb and say he's the one for you. Just trust it."

# Chapter Thirteen

Colton

IT WAS the end of the second period and as I made my way off the ice, I checked behind the bench for signs of Emma, but her seat was still empty. Lorelai waved at me and shrugged as she pointed to the chair that had my jersey hanging off the back of it.

Worry filled me as I made my way to the dressing room. She'd bolted from the room, and by the time I'd run after her, she was already gone. I couldn't take the time I wanted to take and go after her because I had to get to the lobby to catch the bus for the arena. I figured she'd cool off and that she'd show up to the game tonight.

But she didn't.

Unfortunately, after we won the game, and as much as I wanted to return to the hotel immediately, Thompkins insisted I stick around for photographs and interviews, during which both he and Pamela kept a close watch on me, no doubt wondering where the hell Emma was.

After the interview, I was brought back to the hotel and dropped off with the rest of the team. I checked my phone for messages, but there weren't any. I made my way up to our room only to find it in darkness.

I walked back out into the hallway, pulling the door closed behind me, and texted her, then made my way down to the lobby. I strolled through the lobby looking for her. When I didn't find her there, I made my way over to the restaurant. I glanced at the patrons, and then pulled my phone from my pocket, quickly pulling up the group chat with the guys.

I'd just finished typing out the message and was about to hit send when I saw movement out of the corner of my eye over in the corner booth at the back of the restaurant. I made my way to the back of the restaurant and glanced over the booth seat to find Emma sitting there alone, a half glass of what appeared to be pop in front of her.

"Well, well, there you are," I said.

"Here I am," she said, holding her arms out, then giggling.

*What the hell? Was she drinking?*

"What are you doing here?" I asked.

She looked up at me with bloodshot eyes and smiled. "Ohhh, you know, taking a play out of Fox's playbook and drowning my sorrows," she said, picking up her glass, lifting it toward me in a mock cheer before taking a drink.

"How many of those have you had?" I asked, slipping into the seat.

"How many of those have you had?" she mocked in a deep voice, then started giggling followed with a hiccup. "The first, and now the last, does it really matter?"

"Okay, well, I think you've had enough for tonight," I said, reaching for her glass, which she grabbed and moved away.

"So serious," she said, looking up at me.

"Okay then," I said, sitting down across from her.

"What are you doing?" she questioned, looking at me.

"Well, I'm thirsty, so I think I'll join you," I said, waving over a server.

"Are you with this young lady?" the server questioned.

"I am."

"Thank goodness, we were about to call security."

"No need. I will take care of her. Could I please get a soda, and would you be able to get the lady another of whatever it is she's drinking?"

The server looked over at Emma and then at me and shook her head. "I'm sorry, but the lady has had enough tonight. I have cut her off," she said, giving me a nod.

"I see. Well, if I promise to get her out of your hair after this last drink would you be willing to get her even half a glass?" I said, winking, knowing she probably wouldn't even drink them before she was ready to pass out.

"I'm not supposed to do that, but fine." She made her way to the bar, returning moments later with our order, placing the glasses down on the table, and then walking away.

"You are good. All you do is pour a little of that Fox charm on the lady, and she buckles after she'd already cut me off."

"Drink up." I nodded toward the glass, pushing it toward her.

Emma took a sip at the same time I did, then placed the glass down on the table. She leaned against the wall of the booth and closed her eyes.

"What's going on?" I asked. "You always seem so in control of everything."

"I'm in control," she said, picking up her glass again and taking a drink.

I couldn't help but chuckle. "Yeah, right, maybe of the glass in front of you."

"Ugh, now here comes the asshole." She sighed, rolling her eyes. "I told you, a poor attitude isn't a personality trait."

"Can't help it, I guess you just bring that out in me."

God, I loved watching her when she got flustered. Not only was she attractive as hell, just as she had always been, but I swore she was cuter when she was irritated with me than when she wasn't. I could only imagine what makeup sex would be like with her.

"You aren't the only one, apparently," she mumbled.

"What?" I questioned.

She took a drink and wiped her mouth with the back of her hand.

"I said, you aren't the only one. I must attract the bad-attitude gene."

"Why do you say that?"

She avoided my gaze, taking another drink. "I told you I don't want to talk about it."

"Didn't you feel better after you loosened up the

other night and talked to me about things? You need to stop trying to control every single situation and let people in once in a while. Maybe if you did that, you'd stop being miserable as fuck with things in your life, so why don't you tell me what gives. You used to share everything with me."

I could see her thinking through the idea of telling someone her troubles. She was probably so uptight all the time and had pushed so many people away that she probably had no one to talk to.

"It's not my style to talk to others."

"Why not?"

"People talk. They judge."

"And you think by telling me I'm going to tell all kinds of people and judge you."

"You're no different from anyone else."

"How would you know?"

"Because I know people."

"No, you think you know people."

"Trust me, I know them. I see what the media does to people like you."

"That isn't the same thing. They're paid to spread rumors about people. Normal people have better things to do than talk about others behind their backs, and if they are friends, then they don't do that, anyway."

"If only you knew the ones I knew, and we aren't

friends. Friends don't just disappear, especially the ones who claimed that they were in love with you."

While my father had intercepted her letters from getting to me after I'd lost my phone, I guess he'd never sent the ones I'd written to her like I'd asked.

"Okay, then," I said, drinking down the rest of my drink. "Drink up, let's go."

"But I thought you wanted me to—"

"Nope, I want to know nothing. You've made it very clear. Now, drink up."

There wasn't any point in trying to have a conversation about this with her right now. She was far too drunk to try to reason with. I slipped out of the booth and took care of the bill. When I returned to the table, she had her head down, her eyes closed as her head rested on her arm, her phone in her hand.

I carefully slid the phone out from under her hand and noticed it was open to a chat, my eyes immediately drawn to my name. I glanced at Emma, who still had her eyes closed, and then read the last part of the chat.

Chantal: Bullshit, until you met Mark, out of all the guys you dated, all you did was talk about what a loss Colton Fox was when you'd break up with them, and how you wished you could have a second chance.

Emma: Chantal, I did not.

Chantal: You did. Please do yourself this one favor and stop lying to yourself. Perhaps this is life's way of giving you both a second chance.

Emma: You have no clue what you're talking about. Colton would never be interested in a girl like me.

Chantal: Why not? He kissed you didn't he?

I looked down at Emma, her eyes closed as she rested her head on her arm.

"Alright, baby girl, let's go," I whispered, carefully pulling her from the booth and getting her into a standing position as she groaned.

I was more interested in her than she knew, but we needed to sort a lot of our past if there would ever be a chance at a future. I was just after the girl I knew she was, not the one she pretended to be.

"TAKE YOUR SHOES OFF," I said, carefully holding her as I kicked mine off and shut the room door.

She hadn't moved when I looked at her.

"I kissed you...oh God, I kissed you," she said, rubbing her face.

"That you did." I chuckled.

"I don't know what I'm doing. I'm not even over him. If I think about it, I don't think I ever even got over you, and now I've kissed you."

She kicked off one shoe and went to take off the other when she stepped on her other shoe, almost falling. I quickly grabbed her before she fell over.

"Whoa there, baby girl. Be careful."

She looked up at me, bringing her hands to my cheeks. She ran her thumb over my bottom lip.

"You know what?" she whispered.

"What?"

"I enjoyed kissing you more than I ever enjoyed kissing him, and you barely even kissed me back."

"Is that so?"

She nodded and bit her bottom lip.

She was right, I'd kissed her back, but barely, and it wasn't because I didn't want to, but because we were in a room full of cameras.

"Come on, take your other shoe off."

"Trying to get me out of my clothes, are you?" She giggled.

Again, I chuckled. This was so far from the Emma I'd spent the last week with. This was the real one, right here.

"If I wanted you out of your clothes, you'd be out of them," I whispered. "Now take your shoe off."

"Yes, sir." She giggled again, slipping her other foot out of her shoe.

I held onto her and carefully walked her over to the edge of the bed and sat her down.

"Now, I'm going to go get changed. While I'm in the bathroom, can I trust you to change out of your clothes?"

She looked up at me, ran her hand over mine, and nodded her head. "Will you kiss me good night? I'll only do it if you kiss me good night," she said, crossing her arms and looking up at me mischievously.

I let out the breath I was holding. "Fine, yes, I'll kiss you good night. Now, get changed." I grabbed my boxers and went to go to the bathroom when I felt her hand grab the belt loop of my jeans.

"Not so fast. God, I love your ass…" She giggled and then hiccupped. "Hand me my stuff," she said, pointing to the top drawer.

I couldn't help but laugh, while I opened the drawer and looked inside.

"White tank top and gray boy shorts on top of the pile," she said, hiccupping again.

I handed them to her and left her to get changed. When I came out of the bathroom, I expected to find her already changed, but she lay on the bed, passed out, with the tank top on, but she was still in her jeans.

I made my way over to the bed, unsure what to do, but I also knew what it felt like to sleep in jeans, and hers were way tighter than mine. There was no way she'd be comfortable.

I carefully undid her belt, followed by the button on her jeans, and unzipped them, then I slid my one arm under her legs and in one swift motion, lifted her up and slid them off her. When I glanced back up, I noticed she was asleep, so I placed her shorts on the dresser. Then I carefully picked her legs up and turned her, so her head was resting on the pillow and her legs were on the bed, then I sat down on the bed beside her and studied her face.

I should have gone to her when I'd gone to visit my mom, but soon she too moved to Boston. Perhaps had I done that, we'd have caught on to what my Dad had done and we'd have stayed together. God, I felt like kicking myself now.

She let out a tiny whimper, and I reached over and brushed her hair from her face. This was the Emma I knew, the Emma I'd fallen in love with all those years ago. I hoped it wasn't too late for us.

I was just about to get up and make my way to the other side of the bed, when she raised her left arm over her head and stretched out, causing her tank top to raise a little. It was then I caught sight of the top of what appeared to be a tattoo on the front of her hip.

I sat back down, glanced up at her to see she was still sound asleep, and then brought my hand down to the band of her panties. I carefully lowered them and bent down to get a look in the dimly lit room.

There on her hip in red was a heart, and inside that heart were the initials CF. I grabbed my phone, turning on the flashlight, and shone it on the tattoo and ran my fingers over her hip. When the hell had she gotten that? I was about to run my fingers over it again when she let out another moan and shifted on the bed.

Quickly, I shut the flashlight off and made my way around to the other side of the bed and pulled the covers down, then sat down on the edge of the bed. I plugged my phone in, then I lay down, adjusting the pillows behind my head, and stared up at the ceiling. I finally released the breath I was holding and was about to turn over when Emma let out a tiny moan and then another, almost like she was crying.

Instead of rolling over, I spun onto my side, facing her, and shuffled myself until I was in the middle of the bed where I slipped my arm around her waist and pulled her back against me. The instant she was against my body, she let out one more tiny moan and fell into a deep sleep.

As I lay there holding her, my mind racing, the

only question I had for her was about that tattoo, but I never got the chance because when I returned to the room the next morning, she was gone.

# Chapter Fourteen

Emma

PANIC WAS the only thing I could contribute to leaving the away games early.

I'd woken to an empty room and slipped from the bed to find myself in my tank top and panties and my boy shorts laying on top of the dresser.

I didn't even remember coming back to the room. I certainly didn't remember taking my clothes off. The last thing I remembered was talking to Colton in the restaurant, which could only mean one thing: he'd been the one to take my clothes off, and he'd put me to bed.

God, I wanted to die of embarrassment. I never

allowed myself to get like that. Glad to be alone, I grabbed my clothes and made my way to the washroom where I quickly showered and dressed before returning to the room. I'd slipped my shorts and tank top in my top drawer and made my way over to my computer to go through the images and interview from yesterday when I saw a piece of folded paper on my laptop.

I picked up the paper, opened it, and almost immediately my hands began shaking and a wave of embarrassment flooded my body as I stared at the words he'd written.

I swallowed hard, my eyes fixed on his handwriting.

*Can't wait to hear all about that tattoo.*

That was all that it said.

I could feel my heart rate speeding up as I continued to stare at the words he'd written. Then, without any thought, I crumpled up the paper, gripping it in my hand as my mind raced.

A knock on the door quickly pulled me from my racing thoughts, and I heard a woman yell, "Housekeeping."

"Sorry, I'll um, be out of your way in a few minutes!" I yelled out.

"No worries, take your time. I'm sure I can find another room to clean."

I went over to my laptop, quickly emailed Pamela and Larson, letting them know I had an emergency that I needed to tend to, then I quickly packed and left the room. I called a cab and took it to the airport, where I booked my flight back to Vancouver.

I now stood in Colton's living room, eating an apple while I waited for the rental furniture I'd ordered to arrive. I'd figured it would be best for them to drop everything off while we were gone. That way I could stage the house once we returned for the *Off Ice Affairs* interview.

I walked into the kitchen and threw the apple core in the garbage when my phone vibrated. I quickly grabbed it, wondering if it was an update on the furniture, but saw an email from Kerry instead. Dread filled me as I saw the subject line.

There were so many things going on now, I seriously felt as if I were living someone else's life, and to be honest, I wanted to face none of it. To top it all off, I felt like I was failing at the most important assignment of my career, which I'd like to say wasn't my fault, but I couldn't help but feel I was partially to blame.

I wasn't focused; I hadn't been focused since I walked into the room the morning I'd arrived in Vancouver and laid eyes on Colton. No matter how much I'd told myself the man meant nothing to me, every corner I turned said differently. I could tell myself that I was the one with all the control, I could even force myself to try to believe it, but the way the memory of that kiss we'd shared in that interview yesterday had scarred its way into my brain told me everything I needed to know. Or it should have.

I knew why she wanted to talk, so I dialed her number and waited for her to answer. I'd meant to send her an email explaining about the forty thousand I'd donated to the charity, but with everything else on my plate, I'd forgotten, and I knew that the check had probably already hit my account. Which meant that, more than likely, she needed to approve it before they'd clear it.

"Hello."

"Hey, Kerry," I said, taking a breath.

"Emma, finally, listen, we need to have a little chat," Kerry said.

"I agree, and I meant to email you, but I forgot," I replied, sitting back in the chair while taking a sip of water. "It's been an interesting few days."

"Sure has. It certainly was interesting to receive an email late Saturday night for an approval request for a forty thousand dollar check on your spending account without hearing a word from you about it. I tried calling you last night, but it kept just going straight to voicemail."

I thought back to the previous night, vaguely remembering sending her incoming call to my voice-mail when I'd been drowning my sorrows.

I was quiet. I should have emailed her the second I'd written that check and handed it over to Larson; instead, I allowed many things to interfere with my job. I had also allowed my own feelings toward Colton to interfere as well.

"What is going on? I've seen some things in the paper regarding the two of you, and while I understand how the media works, they don't normally drop things this quickly. Need I remind you again how important this case is for the firm?"

"You don't need to remind me. I am on top of it. As a matter of fact, I am just sitting down to go over and approve the interview we ran yesterday morning, which should clear everything up from the fundraising event."

"That's funny, because an article was published a few hours ago from an interview you ran yesterday."

"WHAT?" I said, panic setting in.

"Yes, you two look very happy together. In fact, if I didn't know better, I'd say you two actually were a couple at one point. I mean that kiss...it's also all over Puck-Lit-Love."

I swallowed hard. "That's a good thing, right?" I said, my voice shaking.

"I never said it wasn't. I just don't feel you are taking this seriously."

"Why would you say that?"

"Well, because you've really pulled nothing together that is of any substance to clear his name quicker. His own PR team could have come up with these things."

"Well, I know, and I'm working on that. Mr. Fox can be somewhat of a handful, and while I've come up with something that I know will clear his image and force the media to focus on the good he does for good, he has refused to allow me to use the information for now."

"Emma, you are more cutthroat than this. You just do it."

"Just trust me on this, please, give me the benefit of the doubt. It will come out. It's just a matter of when."

"Don't play games. Why are you not with Colton now? He is at the away games, but I saw the charge on the company card for the flight back to Vancouver."

I closed my eyes. "Yes, you are correct. I had to return because I needed to make sure I was here for the company to come in and stage his house for the in-home interview."

"Right...Emma, I'm not paying you to be back in Vancouver. I'm paying you to be in the presence of

Colton Fox to take care of things regarding your assignment."

"I know."

"Then what are you doing?"

"I promise you—"

"Emma, if you couldn't handle this assignment, you should have told me, and I'd have gotten someone else. Now, I have to go. You need to get your ass back to Colton before this man fucks up his entire career and mine in the process if we fail. I will approve this check, and once you are back in the office in the fall, we will then discuss a repayment plan. Talk soon."

She was gone. I didn't even reply.

I'D WORKED TIRELESSLY for the last two days arranging furniture, unpacking many boxes of accessories to fill the main part of Colton's house. I'd just placed the two blankets on the back of his couch and looked around the properly lit room now.

I was so happy with how the house had turned out. My choices had been perfect, working with the dark colors of his furniture, adding other furniture in the same dark wood tone and mixing it with neutral colours. This space finally had a comforting and inviting look to it.

I glanced at the time. Colton would be back in about three hours, so I got up from where I sat and made my way toward his bedroom. I slipped through his room and into his ensuite and looked over the large inviting jacuzzi tub in the corner.

My body ached the more I looked at it, and I knew that a shower wasn't going to do anything to soothe my aching muscles.

"One bath won't hurt," I whispered to myself.

I walked over, turned the faucets on, and began filling the large tub with hot water. I ran to my room and grabbed my bath salts and then, once it was full, I climbed in and allowed the hot water to seep into my body.

When I'd had enough, I climbed out of the tub and caught sight of my reflection in the mirror, that stupid heart tattoo with the initials CF staring back at me. I swallowed hard.

I could still remember going to get it. I hadn't been old enough to consent on my own, so I'd forged a note from my mother. I knew she'd kill me if she saw it, and so I made sure she never did. It had been a stupid mistake, but then that's what teenagers did.

I ran my fingers over the heart and initials once again. I hated staring at it, for all it did was remind me of how stupid I was to actually think I'd ever meant anything to Colton Fox. I tore my eyes from the mark and looked at my reflection in the mirror. I wanted to die knowing that he'd seen it, and more than ever I needed to find someone who could remove it—sooner rather than later.

I reached over to grab the towel I'd brought in with me when the bathroom door flung open and Colton walked in completely naked.

I froze as my eyes skimmed over his body. The man was immense in every aspect. We both stood there, eyes locked on one another, each of us taking the other in, and then, as if a light switch went off, shock and horror filled me.

What the hell was he doing here? His flight wasn't scheduled to land for another hour yet.

"Oh my god!" I screamed, scrambling to cover myself. "Get out!"

I stepped over and shoved the door closed and then turned to look at myself in the mirror. I'd never be able to look at him again, I thought to myself, mortified that not only had I seen him naked but that he'd seen me.

# Chapter Fifteen

Colton

"WHAT IS THE MATTER WITH YOU?"

"What do you mean?" I questioned, staring at both Dylan and Knox.

When I'd walked through the door, I'd thought I'd been in the wrong house. I actually had to do a double take at my address, so I'd gone down to her room for an explanation for not only the furniture, but the reason she'd left me at the games.

When I didn't find her in her bedroom, I'd figured she'd gone out or something, so I'd gone into my bedroom and stripped out of my clothes, welcoming a hot shower.

I'd walked into the bathroom and was about to flip on the lights when I saw her. She stood there, towel in her hand, staring back at me. At first we just stared at one another. Then she flipped out, screaming, walking toward the door. I'd backed out just in time for her to slam the door shut. Instead of staying and waiting for her to come out, I'd gotten dressed and headed over to Knox's place where I found out that Dylan was still there.

"I don't understand. You should have walked into that bathroom and staked your claim."

"Yeah, man, why didn't you just go in, wrap your arms around her, carry her to the bed, and…"

I stared at both Knox and Dylan.

If this had been any other situation, I'd have done exactly what they were saying, but this was Emma, someone that I cared about.

"I don't know, panicked, I guess."

"Panicked? A guy like yourself, so confident in the bedroom, one who always has girls falling all over him, panicked?" Dylan chuckled.

"Yeah, man, this doesn't sound like the same guy who'd taken on three chicks down in Vegas last summer."

Fuck, I'd forgotten I'd told them that story.

"I don't know. Emma is just…different."

"Oh no," Knox said, pinching the bridge of his

nose before he ran his hand through his hair and looked at me.

"What?"

"Yep, oh no is right," Dylan said, chuckling.

"It's worse than we thought." Knox added.

"What is?" I questioned.

"You really like this girl. That is why you panicked. Not for any other reason."

"Well, there is the history, remember," I said.

"Yes, the history, but I'm not talking about the history. I'm talking about now."

"What about now?"

"Well, you've been acting odd ever since you told us she left the games the other morning. Now this… I'm going to say that it's more than history. I think you might just be in love with her, and if not in love with her, you like her enough that you don't want to fuck things up by taking control."

"I have no problem taking control," I replied, shaking my head.

"Then why are you still here?"

"What do you mean?"

"Well, if you have no problem taking control, you should be on your way back to your place and taking control of the situation before she runs again."

WHEN I RETURNED to my place, the house was dark. I made my way down the hall to find her door shut tight, so I went into my room and jumped in the shower. I checked again before I crawled into bed to see if her light was on under her door, but there was nothing but darkness.

I lay in bed, pillows propped up against the headboard, watching the game highlights from the last few days. My stomach growled, reminding me that I never had anything to eat after I'd gotten home. Without bothering to get dressed, I slipped from the bed and made my way down the hall. I was still in the hallway, in the darkness, when I heard a small moan coming from the kitchen.

I stopped and poked my head around the corner and froze. I was afraid to move for fear she saw me, because what was in front of me, I wanted to watch.

She sat on the kitchen island, in that tight tank top with her foot propped up on the edge of the counter. Her red panties were on the floor at her feet. With her eyes closed and her head back she sat on my kitchen island, her hand between her legs, rubbing her clit. My cock stiffened as I watched her, another almost inaudible moan escaped her.

She bit her bottom lip and pushed her hand back to support her when suddenly she hit the cup behind her, knocking it over. She jumped, stopping the show.

"Oh shit," she murmured and looked toward the hall, probably to make sure she hadn't woken me, and that was when our eyes connected.

She froze, an immediate blush coming to her cheeks. I could see the panic on her face and knew I had to do exactly what my teammates had suggested.

"Don't stop on my account," I said, stepping into the dimly lit kitchen.

Her eyes fell immediately to my hard cock. "I guess you saw…"

I nodded my head, taking another step closer.

"I want to die…" she muttered, turning away from me, but instead of letting her walk away, I walked up behind her and pulled her against me.

I didn't wait, I kissed the side of her neck, my hand running over her perky breast, my fingers playing with her already hardened nipple. I slid my other hand down, between her legs, and ran my fingers through her wet center.

"Watching you get yourself off was the hottest thing I've ever seen," I whispered to her.

She leaned her head back against my shoulder while I continued stroking her.

"I wish you hadn't of stopped. I would have come right there in the hallway."

I took her mouth with mine, then turned her in my arms and lifted her up on the counter.

"Put your foot up," I commanded.

She did as she was told, and I met her mouth, my hand immediately moving between her legs. My fingers danced over her clit, stroking it repeatedly until she moaned.

"I want to make you scream my name, baby girl."

She placed her hand on top of mine, I'm guessing to stop me, but I slid two fingers deep inside her instead.

"Rub your clit for me," I whispered.

Her cheeks were flushed as she bit her bottom lip and looked up at me, hesitating.

"Rub your clit, baby girl," I repeated, as I pulled my fingers from her, adding a third and carefully slid them back inside her.

She cried out. "God, Colton..." she breathed.

"Full?" I questioned.

Her breathing had picked up and the pink hue on her cheeks and heady look in her eyes made me want to take her right here in the kitchen.

"Very..." She moaned.

I met her lips, my tongue washing through her mouth as I pulled her to the edge of the island.

"Wrap your legs around me," I said, my hands supporting her ass as I picked her up.

She did as she was told, and I carried her down the hall and into my bedroom.

"OH GOD, Colton. I'm gonna…come….again…" she cried as she road my cock, reverse cowgirl.

My hands held onto her hips, helping her thrust back and forth, keeping myself deep inside of her.

"Fuck, baby girl. That's it, keep going." I moaned as she tipped her head back.

I could feel her tightening around me for the sixth time tonight. I could feel my orgasm, once again building at the base of my spine. I continued guiding her movements. I loved listening to the sound of her moans as she got louder and louder. I watched as her fists gripped the sheets beside me and her body began to shake.

"That's it, baby girl, come for me," I whispered.

The sound of her moans filled the room as her

body shook and she tightened around me, coaxing the last orgasm out of me.

We were both exhausted, breathless. She groaned as I guided her up and off me to the spot beside me on the bed.

"I'll be right back," I said, quietly and slipped from the bed, returning with a hot cloth for her. which I slipped between her legs, cleaning her gently before throwing it into the hamper.

I crawled back into bed and pulled her against me, and we both fell into a deep sleep.

# Chapter Sixteen

Emma

"I FEEL like we've lost so much time," I said, laying in his arms, my head on his chest.

"I know, but all we can do is move forward."

"What ever happened?" I questioned, lifting my head to look him in the eyes.

"What didn't?" He sighed.

It wasn't something I wanted to talk about, but I needed to know how we went from talking every day to nothing.

"Tell me."

"Well, after I moved away with Dad, things became hell. That was when he started drinking. At first, he allowed me to do whatever, and then as you know he cut my cell phone. Then one night, when I'd gotten home from school, he'd mentioned something to me at dinner about something you'd written in an email, something I'd never told him. He sat there slurring his words, and that was when knew we needed a different way to communicate."

"Yes, we were going to write letters."

"Yes, and I got the first couple you sent, and I responded to you."

"I never got them," I said.

"Yes, and those were the only letters I received from you as well were the first couple. With all that went on with school, practice and my Dad's abuse I figured maybe you decided to walk away from me. I struggled with a lot of things during that time and I didn't have the guts or the heart to find out the truth, so I just let you go, thinking you'd come back to me eventually. Years later, after my father passed away, I found out that he'd hid your letters from me. I found them all in the back of his closet, buried under a pile of boxes. Some had been opened, most were still sealed," he said.

"Why would he have done that?"

"My dad changed after we moved. He kept his word to me, but after he broke up with his girlfriend and lost his job, he became a monster. The only thing I was allowed to do was work and play hockey. He stole from me all the time, taking the money I earned at work."

"I don't understand, why you didn't come see me when you came back to visit your mom? We could have talked it all through and…"

Colton let out a sigh. "It was a mistake, Emma. I should have, but I was so stressed dealing with hockey practice, and then my dad, that when I had time away from him, I just wanted to decompress."

"I'd have understood."

"No, you wouldn't of. I would never have expected that from you anyway. I guess at the time I didn't understand things myself. My dad turned into an abusive monster, and there would have been no way I'd have allowed you to be around that. Just when I was getting ready to move out on my own because I couldn't take things anymore, that was when he gave me the last letter you ever wrote, with your goodbye attached."

"Oh, Colton, had I have known, I never would have written that letter."

"Maybe in some strange way it was supposed to be this way. I mean, maybe, had we of gotten together when we were younger, perhaps we wouldn't have survived."

"Maybe."

"So you read all my letters?"

Colton nodded, and then looked at me, a heaviness in his eyes.

"What is it?"

"Yes, I read them. It was only six years ago or so that I found them. My dad had just died, and my mom was going through cancer treatment."

"How is your mom now?" I questioned, drawing circles on his chest.

"Sadly, Mom died eight months later. Guess they can't cure stage-4 cancer, no matter how much money you throw at it."

"Oh, Colton, I'm so terribly sorry. God, I loved your mom."

"Thanks, but you should know, it was your letters that helped me get through that time."

"Really?"

"Yes. You were the only other person I let into my life long enough to mean anything to me. All your letters, the stories, even though I read them long after they were supposed to get to me pulled me away from the pain of losing my mom. I will say they did remind me of the pain of losing you and that was far different than the pain of losing my mom."

I pressed a tender kiss to his lips. "Thank you for telling me."

"You're welcome."

The room grew quiet as I rested my head back on his chest. We'd been through so much because someone else rewrote our story-, it was hard to be angry now. Now I just needed to accept what had happened to be able to move forward.

"Is that why you got so upset about the cancer foundation?" I asked almost afraid to ask him after his outbreak the last time.

I felt him tighten his hold on me, pulling me against him, like he was afraid I'd leave him once he told me his reasoning.

"I started the cancer foundation. It's named after her. When my mom was diagnosed, she couldn't afford her treatment, so I took it upon myself to pay for it. I'd seen so many people at her treatments, crying because the treatment they were on was no longer working and needed to be changed, but the person couldn't afford the cost. What got me was watching the parents of a three-year-old suffer while their child died because their benefits didn't cover the cost of the drugs he needed. So, after my mom passed, I donated almost eight million dollars and opened up the foundation. I donate half my salary per year to the foundation, and I go there each month to spend time with young kids who are dying."

I lay there listening, not wanting to interrupt, but at the same time wanting to shake the man who'd given me the greatest orgasms of my life only a few short hours ago. He didn't want recognition for what he was doing; he simply wanted to do it and be left alone about it.

"Wow, Colton, that is amazing. You should be so proud of this."

"I know, you are probably wondering why I won't allow you to share this right?" He sighed.

"Yes, I am, but you obviously have your reasons."

"Yes. When Mom died, she asked me to promise her that I'd do something good with the money I earned. She also asked me not to boast about it, to do something that only I knew about so I could feel like I was making a difference, just like I'd done for her."

"What do you mean?"

"Well, my mom, she never wanted my help. She told me that if this was the way it was supposed to be, this was her calling, but I did what I did anyway. I wanted to save her, to have her with me forever. She was the only one who truly cared about me anyway. When she went to thank me, I told her I didn't want the thanks. So, since this was her dying wish, for me to help others without receiving accolades for it, that is what I do. Pamela knows, as do most of the guys, and they respect what I wanted."

"I'll give you that. I asked Pamela and she strongly cautioned me to watch my back."

I felt Colton's chest rise and fall as he chuckled. "Still think you need to watch your back?"

I lifted my head and met his eyes before bringing my lips to his. "No, I don't." He shifted, rolling up onto his elbow and laying me back against the pillow, kissing me hard.

"What do you say we go for another round before I have to leave for tonight's game?"

I couldn't help but start to laugh as he brought his hand down between my legs, gently stroking my already throbbing and sensitive center.

TWO WEEKS Later

THE CROWD ROARED as the Dominators were announced and began skating on the ice. I sat up behind their bench beside Aurora and Lorelai. The moment they announced Dylan, Knox, and then Colton, the three of us stood up and cheered.

We'd barely left the house the past few weeks, aside from games and interviews. We'd created a little love nest in Colton's bedroom and had been happy just spending time wrapped up in one another.

I waved as Colton came skating by holding a jersey in his hand. Tonight, each of the guys in the starting lineup were giving away their jersey to a lucky winner. When he saw me, he skated around and stepped into the players bench, handing me his jersey. He winked and then waited while I lifted his jersey into the air.

The crowd went wild again as I leaned down and kissed him.

I slipped his jersey on over my T-shirt, thankful that he'd decided to give it to me. I'd underestimated how warm I'd be tonight, even with the heat lamps on overhead.

"My god, that was so romantic," Aurora cried.

"Sure was." Lorelai smiled.

I could barely wipe the grin from my face as I pulled the jersey up over my nose and inhaled, the scent of his cologne surrounding me.

"You look so happy," Aurora said, pulling me in against her for a side hug.

"I am," I said, watching as Colton skated past, this time blowing a kiss at me.

"Things also look like they are improving for Colton. Knox wants to know how he can become the next Puck-Lit-Love favorite."

"Him too?" Aurora asked. "Dylan is obsessed with that stupid thing now."

"Sorry, ladies, I feel like that might be my fault."

"No way," Aurora said, giggling.

"Who wants some popcorn and a drink before the game starts?" Lorelai asked, stopping the snack vendor.

We both raised our hands and then sat down together, popcorn in our laps, and watched the game.

THE TWO OF US SAT, curled up on the couch together, watching some TV, when Colton looked over at me.

"What is it?" I questioned.

"Stop me if you think this is a dumb idea."

"Okay."

"Well, I was thinking, I really like what you've done with the place, and it feels like home, so I'd like to purchase all the furniture."

"Okay, that can be done," I said, grabbing my phone and making a quick note to call and put the purchase order through.

"I was also thinking that maybe we could turn the spare bedroom into an office or something."

"Sure, we can do that. After I am gone, of course," I said, smiling over at him, making a note to look into some office furniture. "Did you want a pullout bed or a Murphy bed for when little Mia stays over?" I questioned.

When Colton didn't answer me right away, I looked up at him and saw he was staring at me intently.

"What?" I questioned. "It's an easy answer."

"Um, well, yes, I'd like too, but why do you need to wait until you're gone?"

"What do you mean why? That is where I sleep," I answered.

"What if…we changed that?"

"Colton, I don't think I'm understanding. Where would I go? Or god, are you thinking that it's time for me to leave, because we still have at least one more interview."

He looked at me, a sly smile on his face as he watched me. "That wasn't what I was thinking," he said.

"Okay, well, I guess I can always sleep in the Murphy bed. At least—"

"Whoa, I'm not asking you to sleep in the Murphy bed. I'm saying that we turn the spare room into the office, with either a pullout couch or Murphy bed, and you move in my bedroom with me."

I raised my head and looked at him. I had so many questions running through my mind about what he'd said.

"What do you think?"

I hadn't slept in that room since the night in the kitchen. In fact, I'd already brought all my clothes into his room, and I'd moved out of the other bathroom and into his. I swallowed hard as I looked at him. It was almost already official, but this would confirm what we both already knew.

"I'd like that," I whispered.

"Me too."

He shifted on the couch, making space for me to move in beside him, which I did. The moment I was in his arms, his lips were on mine.

# Chapter Seventeen

Colton - End of November

"FUCK ME. FOUR MILLION VIEWS," I said under my breath as I looked at the screen of my phone. Emma had been right; my face was now everywhere. I'd open up any social media platform and there I was. Shots of me and Emma together at games, out for lunch, even at the park last weekend when we'd gone to the Christmas festival together.

Now as the guys and I sat inside The Sip and Stir having a coffee before we made our way back home, people were taking pictures of us and asking for our autographs.

"She really blew up your career. You are now one of the most loved guys on the team, or at least your relationship is." Dylan chuckled after I took a picture with a young girl who had recognized me.

"Yeah, I know I owe it all to her. Larson is finally off my back as well," I said, taking a bite of my bagel.

"That is good. Honestly, that is the last person any of us want on our backs," Knox muttered.

The interview with Off *the Ice Insiders* had gone so well, they'd spent the day with Emma and me photographing us around the house. They sat down and asked us questions about our relationship, and they even joined us for dinner, which they also took photos of while we cooked together. I was grateful that Emma had coached me on all the answers, because otherwise I was certain I'd have messed them up. They'd even mentioned doing a spread in the coming months on each of the Dominators couples, which Emma thought was a fantastic idea. When they left, Emma promised she'd send them some highlights and information from some of the previous games I'd played this year and had done so immediately after they'd left.

"You're telling me." I chuckled.

The table grew quiet. As I sat here in this small local cafe, I still did not know what we really were to one another. I'd started thinking about that more than a week ago. I'd come home late one night from a set of away games and found Emma curled up in my bed sound asleep. She'd stopped doing the away games and only showed up for the home games like the other girls. I'd watched her sleep for a bit and then crawled in beside her, absolutely terrified of what would happen when all of this was over and she returned to her life. I realized shortly after that I didn't want her to leave; I didn't want to lose another chance at us.

"What is it, big guy? You look conflicted," Levi questioned as he returned from the bathroom.

"Oh, well, now that things are rocking and rolling with my image again, in a positive light, I fear Emma is going to be leaving soon…"

"That doesn't mean it has to be the end," Clay added.

"No, it doesn't, but before she came here, she had a life."

"And you are worried she'll return home, go back to that life, and forget about you," Dylan said.

"Maybe a little. There is a large part of me that'd like her to stay."

I swallowed hard. I was downplaying how I was feeling because the thought of her leaving was doing nothing but consuming me.

"Then ask her, man. Remember our talk about taking control?" Knox questioned.

"Yeah."

"Look where that got you," Dylan said, raising his eyebrows.

"Yeah, hell, I was certain I heard her all the way across the city the other night." Lucas chuckled.

"Shut up," I said, beginning to laugh as the other guys joined in.

I looked at my brothers as they looked at me. They were right.

"Well, now I need a plan," I said, looking at each of them.

"Alright, boys, let's work our magic," Dylan said, leaning forward.

I TOOK hold of Emma's hand as we sat in a quiet corner of Vancouver's newest restaurant, The Crimson Table. Music played quietly in the background as I looked into her eyes. Tonight was so much more than just us. We had things to celebrate because I'd heard from Larson that the charges were being dropped from that horrific night that started all of this.

"That meal was outstanding," she whispered, running her thumb over the back of my hand.

"I'm glad. Apparently, dessert is even better," I said, my eyebrows raising in jest.

"Colton." She giggled, her cheeks flushing.

"What? Seriously, the chocolate mousse is supposed to be out of this world." I winked, which caused her to laugh out loud.

Anticipation of this evening ending was almost killing me. I'd gotten word from Larson that Emma would head back at the end of next week, which had forced me to put together this plan quicker than I'd have liked.

"My gosh…you," she said, her cheeks flushing as she picked up her wineglass.

"Seriously, just wait until I get you home, cover you in chocolate mousse, and lick it off you."

Her cheeks flushed at the thought, and I saw her squirm in her seat a little.

"That would be so messy."

"Yeah, but I have an island that we can work from. That way we don't get chocolate all over the sheets."

Again, her cheeks flooded with color.

"In all seriousness, I just want to thank you for all you have done for me. I know it was rocky to start."

"That it was and now look at us."

"Yeah, I wanted to talk to you about that."

"Oh?"

She looked at me, those beautiful blue eyes dancing, a soft smile on her face as she waited. I swallowed hard; I did not know why I was having such a hard time with this.

"Emma, I know you're going to be returning home the end of next week, or that is the plan anyway, but I've been giving things a lot of thought, and I really don't want you to—"

"Emma? Is that you?"

I looked up to see a man standing there with a couple of other men. He was a good-looking guy, dressed in a well-tailored suit, and then I looked over at Emma, who stared up at him in disbelief.

"Fuck, I just messaged you earlier today asking if we could sit down and talk. I never would have thought you'd still be out here," he said, taking her in.

"Yeah, I got the message."

"Well, why didn't you answer me?"

"Well, I figured it could wait until I returned home."

"Gentlemen, would you mind leaving me for a moment?" he said, looking at the other men he was with.

They nodded and left the restaurant without another word, leaving the three of us there.

I felt like I was in the middle of a terrible movie. I sat there watching the two of them, watching as the looks passed between them. Was this Mark, the guy who'd put her through absolute hell, I wondered.

"I guess it could wait, but since we are here together right now, I just want to say that I'm sorry, and I think we should take some time to sit down and talk when you get back."

She didn't even look my way; she just kept her eyes locked with his.

"I don't know, Mark."

He shifted from one foot to the next, still staring at her. "I think you do. I think you know I'm sorry for the way things went, and honestly, I miss you more than words can say. I made a mistake, Emma."

Emma slowly let go of my hand and dug into her purse for something, but then closed it when she couldn't find what it was she was looking for. "Mark, right now, I think—"

I didn't wait for her to continue; instead; I stood up and straightened to my full height, towering over him. "Mark? Is it? I think you need to leave," I said, looking down into his face.

"Back off, buddy," he said, giving me a shove to the chest.

Emma looked up at him, shocked and horrified he'd just pushed me. "Colton, it's okay, I have it under control," she said, holding her hands out to stop me.

"Oh, so this is him, is it?" Mark said, looking over

at me, a sly smile on his face. "The troublemaker!" he shouted, which caused others in the restaurant to look our way.

"Mark, please stop," Emma pleaded, glancing around at the other patrons watching us.

"Emma, please tell me that you can't be serious. Getting involved with a guy like this, it must be fake. Isn't it?" he questioned.

"Mark, please…" she repeated.

"Ah, yes, I figured you had to be behind the sudden shift in good behavior coming from this guy, all those pretty pictures of the two of you in the fake setting. She is good at her job, isn't she?" Mark said, looking over at me.

Anger erupted inside of me, and I closed my hands, making a fist.

"People should have known it had to be a setup. There is no way a looser like yourself would ever get a girl like Emma in real life."

That was it; that was the straw that broke me. I grabbed hold of him and lifted my fist, bringing it down to his face. The moment my fist connected with his cheek, Mark went flying into a table behind him, the entire thing crashing to the ground. The entire restaurant silenced as Mark lay on the ground, covering his nose and mouth with his hand, and that was when I noticed a camera flash. I looked up to see many people with their cell phones recording us, and that was when I saw Emma staring at me with a horrified look, shaking her head.

Staff came rushing over, helping Mark up off the ground, two men taking him out another door as management followed. Two other servers appeared and began cleaning up the mess of broken dishes, while the other servers distracted the other patrons, getting them to take their seats and ignore what was going on.

I looked at her, pleading with her not to run and to give me a chance to explain.

"What the hell are you doing?" she cried, looking at me. "All our hard work, undone in minutes." She whispered.

I could see the disappointment in her eyes as she looked up at me, and it was then I realized I'd let her down and scared her so badly I doubted there would be any way to earn her trust again.

"Colton, I was going to tell him to leave, and you just got up and went—"

"Emma, I'm sorry. Give me a minute to explain," I pleaded.

Tears flooded her eyes as she stared at me. "I can't do this with you," she sobbed.

"What do you mean?" I questioned, my stomach knotting in fear.

"This, I can't do us anymore. I'm…I've got to go."

She didn't wait. She didn't say another word. She quietly took her things and left the restaurant.

A WEEK LATER

"SHE'S GONE," I muttered into the phone.

I could hear Dylan breathing, so I knew he hadn't hung up on me.

Instead of coming straight home that night, I'd wanted to give Emma time to herself, and I needed to cool off as well. So, I'd gone over to Dylan's for a bit. I'd shared what had happened and then I made my way back home.

I'd figured she'd have been in bed when I arrived home, but the house was empty. I'd thought maybe she'd gone out herself to be with the girls, but in the morning, I noticed all her things were gone. There wasn't a stitch of Emma left in my place, aside from the furniture she'd chosen.

"Sorry, Colton, I really don't know what to say," Dylan said.

"Has Aurora heard from her? Or Lorelai?"

I heard Dylan whisper something to Aurora. "No, sorry, she hasn't heard from her either."

"Thanks, see you tonight," I muttered, hanging up the phone.

Since she'd gone, my life seemed to unravel at a rapid pace. I was once again in the spotlight, first with the events from the restaurant but thankfully the good we'd created quickly wiped out the bad.

I walked into the changing room to see the guys all sitting there, huddled over quietly talking. The minute they heard the door open, they all looked up, a look of unease on all their faces.

"What's going on?" I questioned. "Trouble with the plays for tonight?" I asked, making my way to my locker.

Once I turned my back, I heard whispered words, and then I felt a hand on my shoulder. I turned to see Knox standing right behind me.

"What?" I questioned.

"What you been up to today?"

I frowned. "Slept."

"Ah, have a good nap?" he asked.

"It was alright, why?"

Knox shifted uncomfortably where he stood, giving me an odd grin.

"What is it?" I said, looking over his shoulder at the others.

"You know, Lorelai mentioned you haven't seen her lately for treatment. She really wanted to check your back out before we play tonight. We should head on down there now."

"Oh yeah? When did she tell you this?" I questioned.

"She messaged me ten minutes ago, said she couldn't get ahold of you. Yeah, ten minutes ago." Knox nodded.

I shook my head. These guys were up to something.

"What the hell is going on here?"

"What do you mean?" Knox asked again, shifting from side to side.

"Well, I just saw Lorelai twenty minutes ago, and since when do you dance as if you have pee?"

Knox looked over at the rest of the guys and then whipped his head around at the sound of the locker room door opening. I looked over to see Pamela come in.

"Sorry I'm late, gentlemen," she said immediately, looking my way.

This would explain why none of them had changed, and they all sat around dressed in whatever way they'd arrived in.

"Show me what it is you've found."

"What did you guys find?" I questioned.

"Come on, big guy, let's go get some food," Lucas and Levi both said, getting up from where they were sitting.

Now I was suspicious. Whatever they'd found had to do with me, and I wanted to know exactly what it was.

"Not a chance," I barked.

Pamela turned and looked at me, then put her attention back to the others.

"Go ahead, Dylan, what did you find?"

Dylan looked at me and crossed his arms in front of his chest, then looked at Pamela.

"Well, it's surrounding the big guy here, and…" He paused, looking at me again. "Looks like *Off the Ice Insiders* has found out about Miranda's Miracle Foundation and Colton."

The room spun out of control as Dylan mentioned the foundation I'd created in the name of my mother. How the hell had they learned about that? I'd done everything in my power to keep my name off that foundation, right down to making all these fuckers and the ones in charge here sign an NDA, and then I realized the only other person who knew.

"Don't panic, please. We will get this taken care

of," Pamela said, immediately taking screenshots of the article.

My phone vibrated in my pocket, and when I looked down at the screen, I saw the only person in the world I never wanted to speak to again. How things change, because five minutes ago I'd have begged for a message from her. Now all I could wonder was how she could stoop so low to betray my trust?

In a rage, I whipped my phone across the locker room, smashing it into pieces.

# Chapter Eighteen

Emma - Three Weeks Later

I SAT IN MY OFFICE, looking out over the city. It had been a hellish three weeks. After the publication had gone out regarding Miranda's Miracle Foundation, I'd tried to get in touch with Colton, only he wouldn't speak to me. He wouldn't text me back and he wouldn't return my calls. Soon after, Pamela reached out to me, and I'd come clean with my mistake.

In a rush after the in-home interview, I'd compiled some articles to be printed after their publication. Somehow, I'd accidentally attached the article I'd written about the foundation. The one that Colton had told me I couldn't publish. When I'd seen the article, I felt like I was going to be sick and then Pamela confronted me, I'd explained to her what had happened. I'd expected to hear she was going to call Kerry but instead she surprised me by saying that it was an honest mistake and not to worry.

That was the last I'd heard from any of them. In the weeks that followed I hadn't paid any more attention to anything related to Colton Fox. My heart still ached after what had happened that night at dinner. My heart had wanted to stay and work things out with him, but my mind told me it was going to be impossible for us to ever have a relationship. So, I'd packed up and left.

"Hey, Emma," I heard Kerry say.

I turned around and looked at the doorway.

"Hey, Kerry, you just about done for the holidays?" I questioned.

"Just about. I just wanted to pop in and saw I got a letter today from Kent Cole and from Guy Larson."

"Oh, that is nice."

"Sure is! Don't you want to know what it said?"

I shook my head, afraid that I'd let Kerry down. "No, I don't think so." I sighed, turning back to my laptop, writing my out-of-off email for the holidays.

"Emma? What's wrong?"

That was when I turned around and burst into

tears. "I'm so sorry, I didn't mean to let you down." I sniffled.

"Let me down? You didn't let me down."

"Oh please, I fucked up royally. You should just fire me."

Kerry frowned and then looked at the card she was holding before making eye contact with me again.

"Emma—"

"No really, you should fire me. First, I was an absolute disaster during the entire project, and now the article that went out regarding the foundation should be the final straw."

"Emma—"

"Seriously, Kerry, I should be packing a box, not sitting here writing my out-of-office notification for the holidays."

"Would you—"

"Let you finish. Sure, here, I'll just finish it for you. Thanks, Emma, for the work, continue writing the out-of-office, you'll be employed until the balance of the forty thousand dollars you donated is repaid, and then you will need to find another job. The Image Hackers are ruined—"

Kerry walked into my office and slammed the card down on my desk. I looked down to see the words Thank You, written on the front of the card. Then I paused and looked up at Kerry.

"What's that?" I questioned.

"That, my dear, is a thank you card from Kent and Guy Larson. They wrote to say thank you for doing such an outstanding job. I'd figured you'd want to see it, along with this," she said, placing a check down on my desk.

"What is that?" I asked.

"That is a thank you."

I shook my head, still not understanding.

"It's your tip."

I looked down at the figure that was written on it and swallowed hard. "You're lying."

"No, well, part of it is your tip, part of it is to go back to repaying your debt with the company. The rest is yours to keep."

I frowned looking back down at the check. "Wait, where did this come from?"

"What do you mean?"

"Well, mail call was over eight hours ago, and I know you've been locked in your office all day."

Kerry smiled at me and shrugged. "Maybe you should head on out to the lobby."

"Why?" I questioned.

"Well, because I think there is someone who'd like to see you."

"Who?" I questioned.

"You'll see." She winked at me and left my office

without saying another word.

I MADE my way through the dark office, my laptop bag slung over my shoulder, and stepped into the lobby. At first, I didn't think anyone was there and was about to go find Kerry, when I heard a voice in the hallway. I stepped out the main door surprised to see Dylan and Aurora standing against the railing.

"Hey! What are you doing here?" I questioned, smiling as I hugged each of them.

Honestly, I'd hoped it would be Colton, but given the circumstances, I completely understood why he wasn't here. He probably never wanted to speak to me again.

"Hey, Emma, good to see you. We were asked to bring over the thank you card, and we wanted to see you before we made our way back to the hotel."

"Oh, well, thank you. You guys in town for a game?" I questioned.

"Yeah, tomorrow is the last one, then we head back to Vancouver the next morning," Dylan answered.

"Well, hopefully the last game goes well."

The two of them grew quiet as they looked at me.

"How are you doing?" Aurora questioned.

I shrugged. "Been better," I answered, trying to put a genuine smile on my face.

"If it makes you feel any better, the big guy hasn't exactly been himself either since you left," Dylan said.

I watched as Aurora glanced over at him and shook her head before turning her attention back to me.

"I'm sorry to hear that. I'm sure he's not too happy with me."

Neither of them said anything, which solidified exactly what I thought.

"Why don't you come to the game tomorrow night?" Aurora questioned. "We can sit together. Lorelai is here as well. I know she misses you."

"Thank you, but I have plans tomorrow night," I lied.

"Well, in case you change your mind..." she said, slipping a ticket into my hand. "Just ask for one of us when you get to the arena. They will recognize the ticket."

"Thank you. If plans change, I'll come." I smiled.

Dylan stepped in and gave me a hug, and then as he stepped back, Aurora wrapped her arms around me.

"Don't give up on him. He was so much happier when you were there," she whispered.

I could feel the tears burning in my eyes as she

continued to hug me. I didn't want to give up on him, but I also knew he'd never forgive me for that mistake.

I CARRIED a cup of tea upstairs with me and crawled into my king-sized bed, pulling the covers over my legs. I went to reach for my mug and stopped, picking up the ticket to the game that lay on my night table.

I'd stared at this ticket more in the last twelve hours than I'd done anything else, and here I was again. I should have gotten dressed and gone to watch the game, but instead I decided to stay home. I had to put him out of my life if I were to get over him. Going to see them play, to watch him as he skated around the ice, would only open up the same wound I'd worked so hard to try to close in the last three weeks.

I placed the ticket back on the night table and picked up my mug. I leaned back, took a sip, and closed my eyes, trying to calm my mind. Knowing he was in this city, only a twenty-minute drive from my place, was killing me.

"Fuck it," I said.

I went over to my closet, grabbed a pair of jeans and a sweater, and quickly changed, then I ran down the stairs to the front door. Slipping my feet into my boots, I grabbed my jacket and purse and took off out the front door. I climbed into my car and started the engine.

As I pulled into the arena, I parked around back, just like I would have had I been here with them. I pulled my car into the first empty spot I came to and then made my way inside. When I got to the door, I noticed an ambulance sitting there, lights flashing. They hadn't been there when I'd pulled in.

Frowning, I made my way to the door and pressed the buzzer. A guard opened the door and looked me over.

"Can I help you?" he questioned.

"Yes, I'm a guest of Dylan and Aurora's," I said, reaching into my purse, searching for the ticket.

"Do you have a ticket?" he questioned.

"I do. It's somewhere in here," I muttered, still digging.

As I felt around, I realized I'd left the ticket on the nightstand beside my bed.

"Oh gosh, you're not going to believe this. I seem to have left the ticket they gave me at home. If you could kindly message Aurora, I'd really appreciate it."

He looked at me and shook his head and was about to grab his radio when he held his hand up to ear, pressing on the earpiece he wore, listening.

"I'm sorry, miss. It seems there has been an injury to one of the players. You'll have to wait until they come out."

"Who got hurt?" I questioned, panic filling me.

"Sorry, miss, you're going to have to wait."

"But, please, I—"

"Step back from the door. I'll let you know when we can bring you in," he said, pulling the door closed.

I dug into my purse and pulled out my phone, quickly messaging Aurora to find out what was going on.

> Emma: Hey Aurora, I'm here at the arena, they won't let me in. They said someone got hurt.

I stared at my phone, hoping she responded quickly. It seemed to take forever for those three little dots to bounce around, and then, as I stared at them doing their little bouncing dance that seemed to take forever, she said:

> Aurora: Where are you?

> Emma: I'm at the player's entrance.

> Aurora: Stay there, I'm on my way.

I shoved my phone back into my purse and waited,

wrapping my coat tightly around me. It only took a couple of minutes before Aurora came flying out the back door, looking around until she spotted me. She rushed over, pulling me off to the side.

"Did you hear anything?" she questioned.

"No, why?" I said, starting to feel a little panicked.

"Okay, well, Colton was injured. He's being taken over to the hospital here."

"What? Bad?" I questioned.

"Bad enough. He took a blow to the side of the knee. I am positive it's his MCL. We just need an MRI for a confirmed diagnosis."

It was then the door opened and out came Colton on a stretcher. They lifted him into the back of the ambulance and then turned to look over at us.

"Coming," Aurora said, before she turned back to me. "He'll be alright," she said, placing her hand on my arm before walking away.

"Aurora? Is it alright if I follow?" I questioned.

She looked toward the ambulance and then back at me and nodded.

# Chapter Nineteen

Colton

I LAY in the emergency room, the pain finally easing thanks to the medication they'd given me. I'd had my MRI and was just waiting for the results. Aurora had already gone to see if she could get them a little quicker, when I looked over at the door.

I wasn't sure if it was the medication that was causing me to hallucinate, but I was certain I saw Emma standing there. Then she took a step forward and held her hand up in a small wave.

"Is it really you?" I questioned.

"Yeah, it's really me," she said. "Can I come in."

"What are you doing here?"

She took another small step inside and placed her purse down on the chair on the other side of the room, then took a couple of steps toward the bed.

"Well, last night Dylan and Aurora came over to the office to bring a thank you card, and they gave me a ticket to come see tonight's game. I wasn't going to come but then decided that it might be fun to watch you guys play one last time."

"Alright, but then you'd be at the game?"

"I would be, but when I got there, you were already on your way out and they wouldn't let me in. Aurora told me what happened, so I wanted to make sure you were okay."

"I'm good, just a little knee injury," I said, shifting in the bed, trying to fix the pillow.

"Want some help?" she asked, stepping up beside me, adjusting the pillow behind my back so I was more comfortable.

"Thanks."

"I know you probably don't want to see me, but I couldn't stay at the arena knowing you were hurt," she said, taking my hand in hers.

I looked down at her hand, and then up at her, my eyes locking with hers.

"I tried messaging you after the article—"

I shook my head. "Emma, please…"

Her cheeks flushed as she stared into my eyes. I

wondered if she thought she had crossed an invisible line that could never be redrawn."

"I don't know how we got to this point," she whispered.

I reached over, placing my hand on her cheek. "Listen, I got angry that night at the restaurant. I lost my temper. I am sorry. I lost it again over the article. Had I not broken my phone into literal pieces, I'd have been able to respond to your message before now."

"You mean you would have messaged me?"

"Yes. You see, I never fully admitted to myself how much you meant to me. Having you back in my life made me so afraid of losing you, I held on to you too tight. When I look back on everything, I realize maybe I pushed you away. I did the exact opposite of what I wanted to do. The night Mark showed up, I was about to ask you not to come back here, but to move in with me. The thought of a long-distance relationship made me sick to my stomach because I was so afraid you'd come back here, and he'd get his hands on you and convince you that you should be his, I didn't realize that I'd literally pushed you to him by doing what I did."

"You didn't push me to him.

"Well, that is a good thing."

"I don't think I ever really loved him. Our entire relationship was a lie. Seeing his behavior toward you made me realize exactly what type of man he was. However, seeing your behavior toward him scared me equally. I don't want to be afraid to move around you."

"You don't have to be afraid of moving around me."

The space between us grew quiet as we both sat there looking at one another. No matter how difficult I was, or how much I tested her, something in me still wanted to believe she wanted to be with me. In fact, the more I thought about it, the more I couldn't imagine my life without her. If only I could go back and erase time, especially the dinner where I allowed my emotions to take over, because I regretted everything that happened that night in the restaurant.

"I want to apologize to you. I didn't mean to send the information. It was a mistake, and even though it's one I know you'll never be able to forgive me for, I need you to know how I feel."

"Let me guess, you are sorry?"

She nodded. "I am. You know that I'd never do something intentionally to you when I know how you felt about keeping that a secret."

"I know."

She looked up at me and frowned. "Colton, why aren't you angry with me?" she questioned.

I shifted over on the bed and slid the pillow that was under my knee to support it a little more in my new position, then patted the bed beside me. "Sit down."

The moment she did, I took hold of her hand. "I'm not angry with you."

"Why not?"

"Well, sometimes the things we are afraid of the most have a way of surprising us."

"I don't understand?"

"I had my reasons why I didn't want the news about the foundation shared. I was so afraid of the negative publicity, and I didn't want people asking questions or nosing into my business. Which, honestly, as I look back now, I realize it was stupid."

"Colton, you're reasoning isn't stupid. Please don't think that."

"No, I do, because you were right. Putting that out there changed things for the better. In ways nothing else could change them."

"What do you mean?" she questioned.

"Well, remember when you told me that allowing people to know about the foundation would grow my image?"

"Yes."

"Well, you were right. In the first twelve hours of the article being posted, the foundation had more calls from people wishing to donate. Donations more than tripled, which means more people can get the treatment they need."

"Colton, that is amazing. Your mother would be so proud."

"She would be proud of you, not me." I continued. "With the publicity surrounding the foundation, not only are donations continuing to flood in, but so are the recipients. I learned that people only thought they could use the foundation if they could partially pay for their treatment."

"Colton, that is amazing. You must be so proud."

"No, not completely."

"Why not? What's holding you back?"

"Well, while all the other areas of my life are going well, there is one that isn't complete. The one you were in. I have little to say except…I want you to be with me."

She sat there for a moment, and I wondered if she was thinking about everything like I was, about all the time that had been wasted because we hadn't been together. I didn't want to spend the rest of my life without her.

"So what are we going to do?" I asked.

"Well, you're in Vancouver, I'm here in New York. My job is here. Your job is…well, your job is everywhere." She shrugged.

"Well, I've been thinking about that."

"You have?"

"I have. I'd planned to come and see you before I left. While I don't want you to give up your job, I know for a fact I don't want to do the long-distance thing either. I have been in talks with Larson and Pamela, and they would be more than happy to employ you to come work for the Dominators."

"What? Seriously?"

I nodded.

"When would I start?"

"Well, Pamela said she'd have an opening in the new year, so I'm guessing mid-January."

I could see her thinking it over, trying to decide what she wanted.

"You don't need to give me an answer now," I said, wincing as a sharp pain shot up my leg.

"I don't need to think about it. I know what I want."

"You do?" I questioned.

She nodded her head, leaned forward, and pressed her lips to mine.

# Chapter Twenty

Emma - Christmas Eve

"HOW'S THE KNEE, BIG GUY?" Knox asked as he and Lorelai came into the kitchen.

"Not bad. Your wife there, is a torturous person," Colton said, chuckling as he hugged her.

"Tell me about it." Knox chuckled, coming over and hugging me.

"If anyone wants any wine, help yourselves," I said, nodding to the already poured glasses.

"Can I help with anything?" Lorelai asked, coming over and taking the tray of cheese, I'd just finished over to the table, sliding it into an empty spot.

"Well, did you want to help me with the meat platter?" I asked as I made my way over to the fridge.

"Sure!"

"Baby girl, we are going to join the others in the living room. I'll send Aurora in to help you both."

"Sounds good," I said, leaning in to kiss him before he hobbled into the other room.

Moments later, Aurora, Peyton, Ella, and Scarlett all came into the kitchen and started helping get the rest of the food ready.

"We are so glad you are here," Scarlett said, popping in a tray of appetizers into the oven.

"Yeah, finally we get to meet. I feel like so much has happened since I've been away," Ella said, dumping out some crackers onto a plate.

"Thanks, I'm so happy to be back here with all of you, especially Colton," I said, smiling as I arranged some fruit onto another plate and carried it over to the table.

"Is there much more to do back in New York?" Peyton questioned.

"No, I don't think so. Honestly, I wrapped things up the next day with Image Hackers, and I asked my friend Chantal to help me with clearing out my things from my apartment. She was happy to take most of my furniture, and she was shipping some other things here after the holidays."

"That was nice of her to look after all that."

"Yeah, she knew how important this move was for me. Her and I went to high school together. She was my best friend when Colton and I were together the first time."

"Well, we are going to take you hostage now," Peyton said, giggling. "We should have our first coffee date at Sip and Stir in the new year."

"Oh? What are these coffee dates?" I questioned. "Colton mentioned them to me the other day."

"Oh, you know, just wives of hockey players talking smack." Aurora giggled, as did Lorelai and Emma.

"Just you wait. We all talk about the dirty deeds in the bedroom. It gets rather informative. At times it will feel as if you are sleeping with one of the others," Scarlett said, raising her eyebrows.

"Oh my," I said, my cheeks heating, wondering what I would share when it was my turn.

"Oh, and we never tell the boys, but trust me when I say, I sometimes wonder what it might be like with another one of them." Lorelai giggled, the others joining in.

"You wonder who it might be like with who?" Knox questioned, clearing his throat as he stood in the kitchen door watching all of us.

"Oh, never you mind," Lorelai said, moving over to him, kissing him on the cheek.

"Uh-huh. If you're thinking of joining someone else, I think I might like to know about it. I may have to pull out the magic weapon."

"Well don't pull it out in here." Aurora laughed, then turned to me and smiled.

"Yeah, please, don't pull it out in here," I said, making a face at her.

"Oh, ladies, she is going to fit in just fine," Ella said, grabbing a grape and shoving it into her mouth.

"What do you need?" Lorelai questioned, looking at Knox.

"Well, Colton would like it if you'd all join us in the living room. He has some things he'd like to say."

I wiped my hands on a towel and placed the last plate I'd been working on onto the table, then checked the oven, before we all followed Knox into the living room.

Each of us took a seat beside our significant others. I'd just sat down as Colton stood up.

"Before we eat, I just want to thank all of you for coming and joining Emma and I for our first Christmas together. I also want to thank all of you for standing beside me during this year. It hasn't been my best, and I promise they will only get better as the years go on. Now, hopefully my therapist will have me back playing in a couple months, and I'll be able to help carry the team to victory this year."

"Absolutely I will. That is, if you'll let me treat you instead of whimpering each time I touch you." Lorelai giggled.

"Stop hurting me and I will."

Everyone laughed, and then I watched as Dylan pulled out his phone, holding it up to Colton. When he turned my way, I quickly forgot all about the camera.

"Baby girl. Words can't express how happy I am to have you back with me. I know we didn't get off on the right foot, but now all we have to do is focus on one another. Now, I'd get down on my knee if I could…"

"What?" I gasped.

"Relax, I'm not proposing. At least not yet." He chuckled as he watched the panic wash from my face.

"Okay, goodness, you scared me there."

"Well, just hold on. While I'm not proposing, I am asking for a promise."

I watched as he reached into his pocket. "What are you doing?" I questioned, looking at the others, who all stood there smiling.

"I'm giving you this," he said, holding up a ring I'd recognized but couldn't remember from where.

"It was my mother's birthstone ring. She'd always told me I was to give it to the one until I was ready to buy a ring of my own to give to her. So, I'm giving you this ring as a symbol of my promise to you, that I am yours forever, until you no longer wish for me to be yours."

I held my hand out, and even though I was shaking, he slipped the ring onto my finger and held my hand in his.

"I've loved you longer than I thought, and even though it took us time to come back to one another, I ask that you be gentle with my heart and never leave me."

"Oh my gosh," I heard Aurora gasp.

I looked down at the ring on my finger and then up at those blue eyes I'd always loved and lifted onto my toes to place a kiss on his lips.

"I'll be as gentle as I can," I whispered. "I love you."

"I love you too, baby girl."

The room erupted in cheers as everyone clapped.

"That's it, this is going up for the world to see." Dylan chuckled. "The fans are going to go crazy!"

I leaned in, crashing against his body as he pulled me in tighter and kissed me. Let the fans erupt, I thought. I was ready to burst inside, anyway. I couldn't wait to start this next chapter with him.

## GET A FREE BOOK

Sign up for my newsletter and I'll send you a free book.

https://geni.us/NLSignupBackMatter

# GET A FREE BOOK

Sign up for my newsletter and I'll send you a free book.

https://geni.us/NLSignupBackMatter

What is coming next from S.L. Sterling

To see what is coming next from me visit my website where you can always see the list of upcoming titles that are currently available for preorder.

https://geni.us/ComingSoonfromSterling

Follow S.L. Sterling

Did you know that bookbub has a feature where you can follow me and it will send you an alert when I release a book or put a title on sale? Sign up here and make sure you stay in the loop.

Bookbub:
https://geni.us/SLSterlingBookbub

Website
https://www.authorslsterling.com

Facebook
https://geni.us/SLSterlingFB

Twitter
https://geni.us/SLSterlingTwitter

Instagram
https://geni.us/SLSterlingInstagram

Tiktok
https://geni.us/slsterlingtiktok

Reader Group

Follow S.L. Sterling

https://geni.us/SapphiresReaderGroup

Goodreads
https://geni.us/SterlingGoodreads

Newsletter
https://geni.us/NLSignupBackMatter

# About the Author

An avid reader all her life, S.L. Sterling dreamt of becoming an author. She decided to give writing a try after one of her favorite authors launched a course on how to write your novel. This course gave her the push she needed to put pen to paper and her debut novel "It Was Always You" was born.

When S.L. Sterling isn't writing or plotting her next novel she can be found curled up with a cup of coffee, blanket and the newest romance novel from one of her favorite authors.

In her spare time, she enjoys camping, hiking, sunny destinations, spending quality time with family and friends and of course reading.

To be notified of new releases or sales, join S.L. Sterling's private Mailing List.
https://geni.us/NLSignupBackMatter

Get even more of the inside scoop when you join S.L. Sterling's private Facebook group, Sterling's Silver Sapphires: https://geni.us/SapphiresReaderGroup

His to Hold

Finding Forever with You

**Vegas MMA**

Dagger

**The Doctors of Eastport**

Doctor Desire

Doctor Right

Doctor Frost

All I Want for Christmas (Contemporary Romance Holiday
Collection)

**Willow Valley**

Memories of the Past

The Holiday Dilemma

Letters from the Heart

My Darling Christmas

Scars on my Heart

**The Happy Holidates Series**

Pop Tarts and Mistletoe

Champagne and Fireworks

Summer Nights and Fireflies

**Vancouver Dominators**

Inside the Penalty Box

Ten Minute Misconduct

Crossing the Red Line

Two Minutes for Holding

Playing the Neutral Zone

Through the Five Hole